Tessa's Wishes

Book Three: Whispered Wishes Series

Karen Pokras

Grand Daisy Press

Grand Daisy Press
PO Box 30241
Elkins Park, PA 19027

Publisher's Note: This is a work of fiction. Names, characters, places, and incidents are a product of the author's imagination. Locales and public names are sometimes used for atmospheric purposes. Any resemblance to actual people, living or dead, or to businesses, companies, events, institutions, or locales is completely coincidental.

Edited by Melissa Ringsted of There For You Editing
Cover by Najla Qamber Designs
Models: Courtney Boyett and Willis Totten
Model Photographer: Casey Boyett
Book Layout ©2013 BookDesignTemplates.com

Tessa's Wishes/Karen Pokras. -- 1st ed.
ISBN 978-0-9962843-2-5

For more information, please visit
www.karenpokras.com

"If you wish to be loved, love."

– Lucius Annaeus Seneca

The Whispered Wishes Series

Ava's Wishes
Holly's Wishes
Tessa's Wishes
Woven Wishes
Merry Wishes: An E-book Novella

1

The church sat empty on the morning of September fifth. There would be no guests hurrying to take their seats as soft music played in the background, nor a nervous groom standing at the altar anxiously waiting for his bride to appear through the double doors that seemed so far away. It was a shame, actually, as Tessa had planned everything for her wedding down to the last detail. Included on the list of cancelled items were the string quartet set to play Pachelbel and Wagner as she and her bridal party walked down the aisle, the florist order of white roses and daises, and of course, the three-tiered wedding cake with the bride and groom perched on top, ready to start their happily ever after.

She and Scott had been dating ever since they met in English class the fall of their senior year at Forest Hills University. He was the handsome, popular football star, and she was getting ready for her dream job as the director in the theater school's production of *West Side Story*. Neither of them understood the assignment for the required history class they'd both put off taking until their final year. Perhaps it was coincidence, or perhaps it was fate, but they found themselves waiting outside of Professor Sutter's office at the same time to ask for help. They decided to join forces and work together. Before they knew it, they were a couple.

The pregnancy wasn't planned. Scott did what he felt was the right thing to do and proposed a week before graduation, promising to love and cherish Tessa and the baby for all of eternity. Of course, she said yes. He was her soul mate. The man she was destined to be with forever and always.

They planned to get married in early September. She'd always dreamt of a beautiful winter wedding, but the timing wouldn't work, and she didn't want to wait. If she didn't have her almost perfect white wedding now, she knew it might never happen. A late summer wedding would have to do.

As her belly swelled, so did the arguments, followed by hostility and resentment from her soon to be husband. She rationalized he was just nervous about becoming a father. They'd talked several times about having children when they were dating, and both agreed they wanted a family ... later. Neither had been prepared to welcome a baby this soon. While Tessa was looking forward to the birth of their child, Scott was still having trouble adjusting.

Her family was so focused on all of the excitement going on around them, they didn't notice the trouble brewing. Besides planning for the upcoming wedding and birth for Tessa, her other sister, Holly, had married her fiancé, Ben, only a few months earlier. Their wedding was spectacular—a dream come true for both of them. Then, there was Ava. She and her husband, Max, had recently moved back to the East Coast after having given birth to their second child, Logan. Nobody really saw the end coming, not even Tessa.

In August, two weeks before they were set to walk down the aisle, Scott called off the wedding and moved out of state without saying good-bye or leaving a forwarding address. She attempted to contact his family, but they wouldn't speak to her. She wasn't surprised. They'd wanted Scott and her to put the baby up for adoption from the moment they'd found out about the pregnancy, implying the entire *incident* was a mistake. It was no wonder he got cold feet and ran off.

On Thanksgiving Day, Sophie Rose Haines entered the world. Scott never once called to ask about his daughter.

Three Years Later

"Tessa!" Mr. Abbott bellowed from his office without getting up. "Tessa!"

She quickly put the phone on hold. The fact that she'd been waiting for fifteen minutes to speak with the nurse at her daughter's pediatrician's office was irrelevant. Her boss had made it quite clear on more than one occasion that work came first. Standing up, she straightened her blouse and steadied herself before walking one door over to face the wrath of the man who signed her paycheck.

"Yes, sir," she said, turning the corners of her lips up into a forced grin. Taking a seat in the chair opposite her boss' desk, she braced herself for the inevitable attack.

He slammed the binder down on his desk. "Your projections are off. The return on investment doesn't match the statements, and the interest calculations on the bonds are all wrong. I'm meeting with the client first thing in the morning. I can't present this to him. It's crap! Nicholas Schilling is a multi-millionaire. He pays us a lot of money to get this right ... money I use to pay you. Every time you get this wrong, you're wasting that money."

"Sir, I ran the numbers several times. They—"

"I'm telling you, they're off." Picking up the binder, he held it out as his beady eyes bore through her. "Are you going to sit there and argue? Because one of us is wrong, and it's not me."

There was no use trying to explain. Red would always be blue to him. *Always.*

"Yes, sir."

"These reports need to be completely re-done. All of them. Looks like you'll be working late." He sneered as she took the thick folder out of his hands.

Rising to her feet without another word, she quickly walked out of his office, not giving him the satisfaction of seeing the tears well up in her eyes. *Damn him.* She rushed back to her own office and picked the phone back up. The call had been disconnected. No matter, she wouldn't have time to bring Sophie to the doctor after work anyway. This job truly sucked. Well, not the job itself, but the people she had to work with ... make that person.

Her parents told her she was ridiculous when she announced she wanted to be a theater production major in college. *You'll never be able to make a living doing that.* They were right.

After Scott left and Sophie was born, Tessa moved back in with her parents. She cared for Sophie during the day, while her parents took over at night so she could work as an assistant director at the local theater. She loved the job *and* the people, but barely made enough money to pay her portion of the food bill.

At the same time, her father had just retired, and her parents were looking to sell their house. Initially, when they thought all three of their daughters were to be married off and settled, they had put a deposit down on a condo a few towns over. The place was perfect for them—a fifty-five and older community with lots of activities. Unfortunately for Tessa, it meant she would need to find a new place to live, as her parents would now be in a tiny home that didn't allow young residents. It also meant she was stuck looking for alternative childcare. While her parents would still be close enough to see their grandkids regularly, the hour plus commute would make them too far to be her daily sitter. With rent and daycare expenses now looming, she had no choice but to give up her theater job.

Thankfully, her father had an old college friend, Bruce, a local accountant and financial planner, who was looking for some office help. The pay was decent, and there was a good yet inexpensive daycare close by. She was able to move out of her parents' house before it sold and into her own tiny apartment. Bruce was a kind man who taught Tessa about the business. She found it interesting and learned the ropes quickly. After a year, Bruce, like her parents, decided he was also ready to retire. He sold the business to one of his competitors: Steven Abbott. Mr. Abbott, as he insisted on being called, agreed to keep her on as part of the deal. Unlike Bruce, however, her new boss was not a kind man. He was ruthless ... and heartless.

Tessa constantly had her eyes out for another job. She worried, though. This one was close to Sophie's daycare, gave her basic medical insurance, and covered her rent. And who's to say her next boss would be any better? Although, it was highly unlikely she'd get stuck with someone worse.   She sent out inquiries on a weekly basis with no luck. It looked like she was stuck with Mr. Abbott whether she wanted to be or not.

She began to dial the telephone again.

"Pick up, please, pick up," she whispered just as she heard the familiar *"Hello?"*

"Hi, it's Tessa. I need your help."

2

"Tessa? What's up?" Ava sounded flustered when she answered the call. In the background, her son, Logan, was shouting for her ... crying was more like it, drowning out any silence that might have existed prior to the phone ringing.

At three years old, he was a typical toddler, always wanting attention, particularly when his mom was in the middle of something else. By the sound of it, if Logan didn't get what he was yelling for that very second, his world would surely come crashing down around him.

"Sweetie," Ava said, with more than a hint of pleading in her voice, "I just need to talk to Auntie

Tess for a minute. Tessa, would you mind holding on for a sec while I get him settled?"

"Sure, no problem," she replied.

The click of the television turning on drowned out his demands. Too many times, she had done that herself, trying to distract Sophie with a show or movie so she could get something accomplished, or to squeeze in some much needed alone time. *Parenting at its finest.* She knew it wasn't the best alternative, but often she had no choice, and it wasn't doing anyone any harm … was it? They did plenty together. Besides, Sophie loved her shows. Logan probably did as well. It's not like she put her daughter in front of the television for hours at a time. At least, not very often.

Dealing with one young child was challenging enough. Tessa couldn't imagine what it was like for Ava to have two, although at almost eight years old, Jenna was hardly a young child anymore. Come to think of it, she was probably a big help to her mom. Plus, Ava had her husband, Max, to support her both emotionally and financially, even if his job as an airline pilot did require him to travel often. The fact of the matter was that Tessa would gladly switch places with her older sister any day, even with the sacrifices Ava had to make moving back to Forest Hills three years ago.

Her oldest sister had always dreamt of owning an art gallery, and she was so close to making that wish come true. When she and Max lived out in California, she ran a gallery, quite successfully. The owner had been all set to sell it to her, but Ava found out she was pregnant with Logan. Not that having a child was bad news or anything. Quite the opposite, in fact. She and Max were thrilled. It's just that she'd had such a difficult pregnancy with Jenna and a hard time balancing her time between being a mommy and having a career. After giving it much thought, she turned down the offer and selflessly decided she wanted to devote all of her time to raising their kids. She and Max packed up their children and moved back to the East Coast so they could be closer to both of their families. She hadn't stepped foot in an art gallery since. She claimed she's had no regrets. Tessa wasn't entirely convinced.

Maybe they weren't so much sacrifices, as they were changes in plans. In reality, had any of their lives turned out as intended? Perhaps Holly's had, although to date she didn't have that house full of kids. It's possible, though, after hanging out with her sisters' kids, she had changed her mind or was in less of a hurry. Even so, Holly still *could* have kids. It's not like she was giving anything up. Everything else in her life was going forward right on schedule.

No, Tessa was talking more about long-term objectives, like her desire to run a theater and perhaps get married. She'd already attempted to work in a theater *and* get married. Both undertakings had been dismal failures. The theater didn't pay, and ... well, men sucked. She'd said it a million times over the years to her sisters every time she watched them go through heartache. True, they were both happily married now, but the thought of going through the kind of pain she went through with Scott again to *maybe* find a partner was a crap shoot she wasn't willing to gamble. She was perfectly fine with being single. She could even handle a life away from the theater. Now her crotchety bastard of a boss was another story. He had to go. He was more than a sacrifice, he was cruel and unusual punishment. Oh, how she wished she could find another job.

"Tessa? Are you there? What's up?" Ava asked, returning to the phone.

She hated to ask her older sister for yet *another* favor, especially when Ava sounded so worn out. After hearing her voice, Tessa wished she could have made up some small talk, hung up the phone, and called Holly to ask for help with Sophie, but she already knew Holly had parent-teacher conferences after school today and would be unavailable. It seemed like she was always asking one of her sisters for help, but this was an emergency. Well, not an emergency in the sense of life or death, but an emergency in the sense that if she didn't finish this project, she could lose her job. No, she would most definitely lose her job. If that happened, she and Sophie would have to move in with her older sister. *Ask Ava for a favor or move in with*

Ava? Yes, the favor route was definitely the better choice in this situation.

"I'm here," she said, keeping her voice low in case Mr. Abbott was eavesdropping, as he often did. "Listen, I'm so sorry to ask you this, but my boss is being a royal ass, and I have to work late *again.* Any chance you can pick Sophie up from daycare and give her dinner? It looks like I'm going to be stuck here a while." Holding her breath, she cringed as she waited for her sister's response.

"Sure." Ava sounded exhausted as Logan broke out in full-fledged hysterics. Apparently television was not an acceptable substitute for what he wanted.

Letting out a long breath, she closed her eyes for just a split second in relief. "Thanks, sis, I owe you one. I'll call you later. Give everyone a kiss from me."

Swiftly hanging up the phone before the guilt set in, Tessa tried to blink back her tears. *Ava always said yes ... even when it was a burden.* Bringing her hands up to her eyes to brush away the few drops that had managed to escape, she returned her attention to the client folder sitting on her desk.

"Tessa!" Mr. Abbott hollered from his office. "Those reports are not going to get done if you're busy gossiping on the telephone with your girlfriends!"

Seriously? She'd been on the phone for all of two minutes. Was he expecting her to respond? Apologize? Argue? Grovel? Just what exactly made this man so miserable day in and day out? She didn't care. Her patience had left the building hours ago, and she had no interest in psychoanalyzing the psycho in the next office. Instead, she stuck up her middle finger, watching her doorway to make sure her asshole boss wasn't standing there, of course. Feeling slightly better, she picked up the binder and began flipping through the pages of the Schilling file.

3

Tessa stared at the numbers on her computer screen. How could they be wrong? They weren't. She'd used the same formulas and broker statements as she had every quarter for the past two years. All of the checks and cross-references were formulaic and in place. If she'd entered a wrong number, they wouldn't tie back correctly to the statements. The reports were foolproof. A method she'd tirelessly perfected last year, not that her boss had bothered to notice or appreciate the hard work she'd put in to streamline the process. To him, the fact that she was able to create reports in less time didn't mean she was being more efficient. No, to her cranky old-school boss, it meant she *had* to be rushing and therefore was *obviously* not doing a good enough job.

Added to that, Mr. Abbott was in a bad mood, *again*, and his moods seemed to be getting worse. This wasn't the first time he'd thrown the binder back to her, but usually she had a day or so to let him simmer down. She'd tweak some of the formats and colors in her charts, careful not to disturb any of the actual calculations, and present it all back to him ... during her regular working hours. He'd give her some line about how if she got the numbers right the first time, she wouldn't have had to redo everything. She'd smile, say, "Yes, sir," and be on her way. Tessa could handle that routine. *That* routine didn't take her away from her time with Sophie. Lately, however, he seemed to get a kick out of making her work late. Him and his damn ego—did he really think he could push her around like that? Apparently so, as here she was working past six o'clock yet again.

Having done all of the usual insignificant changes, she pondered just how long she should sit in her office, pretending to work before printing out the *new* reports for her boss. Judging by his current phone conversation, she'd have to add a few minutes to let him cool off before approaching him.

"I don't give a rat's ass. I'm tired of your excuses. Either get the job done, or I'll find someone who can."

She cringed as she listened to his temper tantrum through her office walls. At least he'd moved on to screaming at someone else. Wondering who it was and what they'd done to piss him off, she settled back into her chair and closed her eyes, blocking out the sounds and grateful for a moment of reprieve. Ava had most likely picked Sophie up already. If she left in the next twenty minutes, she could probably get her daughter before they started eating dinner.

"Tessa!"

Startled, she sat up straight. Her boss stood in her doorway, looking annoyed as usual.

"I'm not paying you to sleep on the job."

"I'm not sleeping, sir, I was just—"

"Save it. I'm heading out for the night. I expect those reports to be fixed and on my desk when I return in the morning. I'm meeting with Nicholas first thing in the morning. If he's not happy, I'm not happy. Do you know what happens if I'm not happy?"

"Then I won't be happy?" she meekly asked.

"I don't pay you to be happy. I pay you to work. Get it? Lock up when you leave."

His eyes, already small and full of anger, shrunk even more as he squinted into a purposeful glare, before sharply turning away. Without another word he was gone. The front door to Abbott and Associates slammed shut behind him on his way out.

"Actually," she muttered, "you're not paying me at all at the moment, since I get the same salary whether I leave at five or work all night long. Lord knows you're too cheap to give me any overtime."

Through her window she watched as his over-priced, mid-life crisis sports car raced out of the parking lot. What made Nicholas Schilling so special anyway? He was just some stodgy old businessman who happened to have a lot of money. So much money, in fact, that he paid an outrageous sum for her firm to keep track of it all. She could keep track of her own funds in about sixty seconds flat. Big deal. Money wasn't everything. She clicked print to get the reports started.

Sitting at her desk as the paper started to feed through the machine, she felt even more hostile toward this man she'd never met. *Rich old bastard.* The quarterly meetings were always held at his office in the city or some other fancy locale. He was apparently far too important and busy to come out to Forest Hills. Mr. Abbott didn't seem to mind and always made it a point to bring Schilling's favorite scotch and cigars with him. *Scotch and cigars for a nine a.m. meeting? Nasty.* Thankfully, she wasn't ever asked to attend. She wanted no part of their snooty boy's club bonding.

While Tessa checked her email, the printer continued to hum. Junk. Always junk. She'd sent out a fresh batch of resumes this week, including one to a tiny theater looking for a full-time financial manager. It wasn't her ideal position, but it got her closer to the stage and paid enough to cover her bills. More importantly, it took her away from this place. Unfortunately, she'd yet to hear a response to that or any of the other jobs she'd applied for. The job market was a tough one these days.

Screeching out a piercing beep, the printer came to a grinding halt.

Damn. Walking over to the machine, she began the arduous process of opening and shutting compartments, trying to figure out exactly where the paper jammed. When was Mr. Abbott going to get that new printer he kept promising? *Never. He was a cheap bastard.*

After no less than an hour and a half of printer wrangling, Tessa finally placed the finished reports on her boss' desk. The charts looked completely different, but the numbers were exactly the same. He'd never notice. *Idiot.* She grabbed her coat and purse, hoping to get to Ava's house before Sophie passed out on the couch. All she'd wanted was some quality time with her daughter, and now her entire night was ruined; wasted on trying to please old man Abbott, money-bucks Schilling, and a temperamental printer. Just as she reached the door to leave, the telephone began to ring.

"The machine can pick it up," she mumbled before realizing she'd forgotten to turn it on. Sighing, she reached for the phone. "Good evening, Abbot & Associates," she said, hoping it wasn't her boss checking up on her.

"Oh ... hello," the deep voice said, sounding surprised. "Sorry, I wasn't expecting anyone to still be there. I was just going to leave a message. Is Steven Abbott in by chance?"

"No, he's gone for the day. Can I help you with something?"

"Yes, this is Nicholas Schilling. Tell Steve I apologize for the late notice, but I'm afraid I'm going to have to cancel our meeting for tomorrow. I'll be out of town for the next few days and will call to reschedule when I get back."

Hunching her shoulders forward, Tessa shook her head in frustration. "Of course. I'll leave him the message, sir."

"Thanks, and again, please apologize to him for me. I hope cancelling on short notice like this isn't too much of an inconvenience for anyone."

"No, it's no problem at all," she lied, as she scribbled a quick note on the pad of paper that sat at the front desk.

"Thank you. I'll be in touch." He abruptly hung up the phone.

"Nope, it's no problem at all," she repeated as she slid to the floor and began to cry.

4

Shortly after nine o'clock, Tessa pulled into Ava's driveway. She sat for a moment, listening as the crickets chirped amongst the rustling leaves, and rested her head on the steering wheel in pure exhaustion. The sound of a passing car brought her out of her drowsy state. Shaking her head to wake herself up, she grabbed her keys and headed toward the front door.

"Is she asleep?" She softly walked over to the couch where Sophie was curled up with her favorite blanket and doll, both gifts from Tessa's parents when she was born. Three years later, her daughter never let them out of her sight. The pink and purple blanket, frayed in several places, but soft as anything from having been washed so many times over the years, Sophie had named *Biddy* back before she could even say Mama. The doll she called *Daisy,* most likely for the flowers on her dress that were once vibrant, but were now barely recognizable.

"She had no interest in dinner," Ava said, brushing the hair off her eyes. "And passed out shortly after we got home. Her teacher said she seemed kind of out of it." Resting her hand on her forehead, she looked at her niece with concern. "The fever just started, but I didn't want to wake her to give her anything. I knew you'd be here soon."

Tessa nodded, trying to act surprised that her daughter was sick. The truth was, Sophie hadn't felt well that morning either. In her heart, Tessa knew she should have kept her home, but the reality was she couldn't. The big Schilling meeting had been on tap for tomorrow, and even though she'd had the reports done correctly and on her boss' desk way ahead of schedule, *the first time,* she had a feeling he'd find something to complain about. *He usually did.* All that aside, however, the reality was that she was out of personal days. Mr. Abbott wasn't one of those bosses who just shrugged and said, *"Aw, your daughter's sick? No problem, take the day off."* Or even, *"Take the day, but I'm not paying you."* No. He was one of those bosses who said, *"If you don't show up, don't bother coming back."* The fact that she worked more than her share of hours this week was completely irrelevant. She really needed to find a new job.

Putting her hand to her daughter's forehead, she felt the heat radiating off it before even making contact. *Crap.* There was no way she could send her to daycare tomorrow. But who would stay with her when she went to work? Ava had already gone above and beyond. Tessa didn't feel right asking her for another favor. Holly was out of the question as she worked full-time, and her parents were away on a two-week cruise. *Damn you, Scott. You should be here sharing the responsibility.*

"Are you hungry?" Ava asked. "I can give Sophie some medicine, and she can rest here for a bit longer. I've got chicken left over from dinner. Or, I can make some tea if you just want to unwind a little."

Tessa was both stressed out and hungry. Starving, in fact. She hadn't eaten anything since lunch, if you even wanted to call it that. Technically, she was supposed to get an hour lunch every day, but she rarely took one. Mr. Abbott usually scoffed at her if she left her desk to even use the restroom, let alone leave for lunch. Her afternoon *meal* generally consisted of stale coffee, a power bar, and an apple at her desk while her boss was out at one of his own fancy lunches—at which time, she wasn't *allowed* to leave the office. God forbid she left the phones unattended, she'd never hear the end of it. Still, food was the last thing on her mind at the moment.

"Thanks, but I think I should get Sophie home. It's been a long day." Picking up the daycare bag, she slung it over her shoulder and gazed at her daughter. She looked so peaceful with thick dark lashes covering her closed eyes. Her breathing was calm, almost melodic, casting a spell over Tessa as she watched the dark curls turn into waves that framed her beautiful yet delicate features.

"Are you okay?" Ava asked, disturbing the trance. "Do you need help carrying her out to the car?"

"No, I'll be fine. I just want to get her to bed." Gently lifting her daughter up to her shoulder, Sophie clutched her doll and blanket even tighter as she nuzzled into Tessa's neck. She stopped to savor the warmth of her daughter's closeness. It brought her a comfort no man had ever been able to duplicate. Her daughter may not have been planned, but Tessa couldn't imagine a life without Sophie in it. "Thank you for picking her up, I hope it wasn't too much trouble."

"It's never too much trouble." Ava smiled at her. "Sophie's family."

Was that a look of understanding or pity?

"I hope she feels better. Will you call me tomorrow and let me know how she's doing? I'm assuming you'll keep her home?"

Looking at her sister, Tessa nodded and noted how carefully worded that last sentence was. It purposefully lacked an offer to help. She didn't blame her sister. As much as Ava loved Sophie, she had her own two children to think about first. Keeping them healthy was most likely on the forefront of her mind.

"Yes. Hopefully my boss will be okay with me working from home. I mean, he's just going to have to be." *Either that, or I'll be out of a job. Guess I'll find out in the morning.* She tried to force a smile as she headed toward the door. Sophie moaned in her sleep as Tessa moved. "It's okay, baby," she soothed. "We'll get you home and to bed in just a few minutes." As Tessa reached down to get her daughter's coat off the couch, the bag on her shoulder slid down her arm, bumping Sophie in the leg.

"Mama, I hurts," she whimpered softly waking up with tears starting to stream down her face.

"I know, sweetie. I'm sorry. Let's go home and get you all better."

Ava followed her sister out to her car and helped to get Sophie buckled safely into her seat, despite Tessa's earlier protests that she didn't need assistance. Sophie was back asleep with her blanket and doll secure in her arms within seconds.

"Promise to call me tomorrow, okay?" Ava asked, eyes full of worry.

"I will, promise." Sliding into the front seat, Tessa checked behind her to make sure her daughter still looked comfortable before starting up the ignition.

5

Twenty minutes after Tessa finally fell asleep, the crying started. It wasn't full-blown screaming, like when Sophie was having a nightmare, it was more of a constant sob, mixed in with a horrible wheezing sound ... and it didn't sound right. A mother's intuition was never wrong.

Stumbling out of bed, Tessa wearily made her way to her daughter's bedroom. She didn't have far to go. Their two-bedroom apartment was more like a one-bedroom that had an extra wall put in as an afterthought to create the additional room. She'd had more space in her tiny college apartment.

"I'm here, baby," she said, padding her way through the dark, past the stuffed toys and piles of laundry strewn on the floor toward the sounds coming from her daughter.

Tessa cradled Sophie in her arms, trying to get her to sit up in hopes of helping her breathe a little better. Her eyes remained closed. Was she still asleep? Her daughter's cheeks were bright red, while the skin underneath was ashen grey, not the beautiful porcelain color everyone always raved about. The temperature coming off her neck was red hot.

"Mama needs to grab the thermometer and a cool cloth for you. I'll be right back." Kissing her daughter on her forehead and propping her up against some pillows, she tried to think if her skin had ever felt so warm before. Sure she'd been sick in the past, but never so hot and lethargic. And she'd never heard wheezing like that as far as she could recall.

Coming back quickly, Tessa draped the wet towel across Sophie's head and waited for the familiar beep from the thermometer already in her ear. Within seconds, she pulled it out and blinked her eyes as she looked at the number on the display. Hitting clear, she placed the tip back in her daughter's ear a second time just to be sure. Once again it beeped, and Tessa read the number. One hundred and five point five. *Twice.* There was no mistake. She'd given Sophie a dose of fever reducing medicine just an hour before. Her temperature should have been going down, not up. She wrapped her daughter in her blanket, made sure she had Biddy and Daisy, grabbed her own purse and keys, and headed out to the emergency room at Crestmont Memorial Hospital.

The E.R. was packed, but they took Sophie back to a triage room right away. Over the next hour or so, several nurses, medical students, and interns came in and out of their room—asking questions, looking, examining, taking vitals, and poking. Poor Sophie. All she wanted to do was sleep. All Tessa wanted was some answers and something to help her daughter get better ... *fast.*

So much for getting called back to a room quickly. They would have been better off being left out in the waiting room to rest. The doctor on call still hadn't seen them yet. She tried to lay Sophie down on the bed in the room, hoping she would get some sleep, but she only wanted her mama to hold her in an upright position. Managing to get up on the exam table with her back against the wall and her daughter resting on her shoulder, Tessa felt her eyes getting heavy.

She woke with a start an hour and a half later as the curtain to their room screeched open. A man in a white lab coat, holding a chart, introduced himself as the doctor. The real doctor—not the med student or the intern—but the person they'd come to see almost three hours ago. Tessa was so annoyed at the fact she'd been waiting so long, she didn't bother to pay attention to his name, nor did she accept his handshake. She merely stayed on the exam table and waited for him to do whatever he needed to do to help her daughter.

Quickly looking down to his chart, he scanned it before starting to speak in a rushed voice. *Great. He's going to look at her for thirty seconds, say she's sick, and send us on our way. In ten days, I'll get a bill. Awesome.*

"It seems your daughter has the flu, Mrs …" The doctor flipped through the chart, apparently looking for Tessa's last name.

"It's Miss," she replied with an irritated tone. Why did they always assume? "Miss Haines."

He looked up. Was that a smile? Surely he wasn't hitting on her in the middle of the night when she was there holding her sick child. *Ugh!* So what if he was swoon-worthy with piercing blue eyes and a perfect three a.m. stubble. She was way too peeved about the wait and only cared about getting Sophie better.

"… and she had the flu shot. She gets it every year," she added, still aggravated. Between a stressful day and evening at work, a sick child, and now sitting in this room for hours, she was completely out of patience.

The doctor closed his chart and examined Sophie as Tessa held her, listening to her heart and lungs, and checking other vitals, before hopping up on the exam table to sit next to them. Tessa slid down slightly to move away.

"You didn't hear this from me," he said, leaning into her, "but the flu shot is kind of worthless, at least this year. The manufacturers of the vaccine have to try to figure out which strain of the flu will hit months before the shot goes into production. This year they didn't even come close to getting it right. We're seeing more and more cases of it every day. Especially in little ones."

"Fabulous," she sighed, rolling her eyes. Sophie moaned as she nodded off again, placing her head back on her mom's shoulder. At least she was getting some rest. "So, how long until she's feeling better?"

"It's hard to say," he responded. He reached his hand to push Sophie's hair out of her eyes and felt her forehead. "You were smart to bring her in. We can give her something for her fever and an anti-viral medication that has had some success in helping to relieve some of the symptoms when it's caught early, as in this case. The good news is the vaccine sometimes lessens the duration of the virus even if it doesn't prevent it. She'll be fine in a week or so. It just has to work its way through her system. Make sure she gets plenty of fluids and lots of rest." He hopped off the table and pulled a prescription pad from his coat pocket.

A week or so? I'll be unemployed in a week or so!

"Are you okay, Miss Haines?" he asked, looking at her. "You look a little pale."

Taking a deep breath, she tried to control her breathing. *Now is not the time to have a panic attack, Tessa. You have to think about Sophie.*

"I'm fine," she said, in a final long breath as she felt her heart beginning to self-regulate. She'd been in worse situations than this and survived. *She was Tessa Haines. The fighter. The one who didn't take crap from anyone. The one who was unbreakable.* She took the prescription from the doctor and was thankful she made it home before the tears began.

6

T essa nervously tapped her fingers on her kitchen table as she listened to the phone ringing through her receiver ... one, two. She knew he would be in the office early as he would have had to pick up the reports for his meeting with Nicholas Schilling. Maybe he hadn't seen the note and left? Three, four ...

"Steven Abbott," the brusque voice finally answered.

She let out the breath she'd apparently been holding.

"Good morning," she said, trying her best to sound like a confident professional despite the fact that her heart was beating so loud she could barely hear her own words. "It's Tessa. Did you see my note about Mr. Schilling? And my reports?"

"Yes," he replied.

She waited. No, "*Thank you, Tessa. I so appreciate you working your ass off late into the night even though the client cancelled.*" Or even a gruff, yet simple, "*Thanks.*" Did she really expect one?

"Well, um, my daughter's sick. We were at the hospital until early this morning. I don't think I'm going to—"

"I've already spoken to Nicholas," he interrupted. "We're meeting next quarter. The reports will have to be completely revised to reflect new projections. There's a lot of work to be done. Find someone to watch your kid. I expect you here in thirty minutes." He hung up the phone before she could respond.

Closing her eyes, she sighed. What did she expect? "*I'm so sorry, Tessa. Of course you should take the day off to be with your daughter. In fact, you worked so hard, let me pay you for the day. You deserve it. The important thing is that your daughter gets better.*" No, that's what Bruce would have said. Not Mr. Abbott. He said exactly what she would have expected. Except, there really wasn't any work to do today for this client. Three months out was too early to make any new projections. She needed to wait at least a month or two to see the trends in the market, plus she would have to gather all new broker and bank statements to get an accurate picture of his portfolio.

Those wouldn't even be available yet. The truth was, Tessa normally waited until the week before these meetings to drop her numbers into her formulas and then tweaked them a few days before. Who could really predict the market? If it were that easy, she'd be a rich woman. All she really had to do today was catch up on work for the other clients she'd neglected while working on the Schilling reports. And those could wait another day or so. There was nothing pressing, and he knew that. Regardless, she knew trying to explain that to her boss would be a useless effort. He was just being spiteful.

Twenty-five minutes. That's all she had to get in there before she was most likely fired. She flipped through her checkbook. At most, she had two weeks' worth of income saved. Would that give her enough time to find a job and cover her bills if she walked today? She knew the answer before she asked herself the question. To make matters worse, that savings would most likely go to pay for last night's emergency room visit, since Mr. Abbott's cheap medical plan wouldn't cover much of it. She peeked in at Sophie, still fast asleep in her bed. At least her fever had dropped. It was still above a hundred, but one hundred and one was much better than one hundred and five point five.

Ava would probably agree to watch her. She always said yes, but Tessa didn't want to ask her again or risk getting Jenna and Logan sick. Holly was at work. Plus, she doubted she could get Sophie up and over to either of her sisters' homes and still make it to work on time. With no other options, she walked quietly over to her daughter's bed and ran her fingers through her soft curls.

"Sophie, sweetheart, it's time to get up. Mama needs to go into work."

"Mmmm," she moaned as she rolled over, hugging her doll and blanket even tighter.

Grabbing Sophie's daycare bag, Tessa filled it with toys and activity books, and went back over to her daughter.

"Soph?" she tried again. "Mama's going to go get dressed, and then we need to go, sweetie, okay?"

"Mmmm hmmm," she mumbled, still not opening her eyes.

Taking the bag into the kitchen, Tessa added juice boxes, snacks, and the medicine the doctor from the hospital had prescribed. She'd forgotten about him until that moment. The hospital had given Sophie her first dose of meds right there in the emergency room, and when they were finally released, they stopped at the pharmacy window on the way out to fill the prescription. She turned the bottle around to study the label. So Dr. Swoon-worthy apparently had a real name ... Dr. Brandon Hall. Placing the bottle in the bag with everything else, she checked the time. Twenty minutes.

She quickly downed a cup of coffee, got dressed, grabbed Sophie, Biddy, Daisy, a small quilt off Sophie's bed, a pillow, and the bag. Loading them all into her car, she headed into her office.

Mr. Abbott scowled as Tessa walked in with Sophie in tow, the two of them carrying what looked to be half of their apartment in their arms. All he said was get here in thirty minutes. He didn't say anything about what she could or couldn't bring with her. Judging by the time on her watch, she had three minutes to spare.

"Tessa!" he hollered as predicted. "My office—now!"

She spread out the quilt and pillow on the floor of her own office and gently placed Sophie down with her toys. "I'll be right back," she whispered, giving her a kiss.

"Yes, sir?" Tessa asked innocently, walking through his doorway and taking a seat in one of his leather chairs.

"Do you mind telling me what's going on here?"

Be strong. Don't let him bully you. Smile. "I told you," she said sweetly, trying to calm him down, "my daughter is sick today. I'm afraid she can't go to daycare. I tried to explain earlier that—"

"And I told *you* to find someone to watch her."

Okay, maybe the nice approach isn't going to work.

"Well, I don't have anyone, so it was either bring her in or stay home, and you made it clear that staying home wasn't an option."

"Mama! Mama!" Sophie cried from the next office. "Mama! Mama!" She came running into Mr. Abbott's office holding Biddy. "My tummy doesn't feel good."

Tessa watched as her daughter's face turned a shade of green she was all too familiar with. Jumping up, she grabbed the trashcan from under the desk just as Sophie vomited into it.

"Ugh. Vile!" her boss moaned, turning his head. "Go on. Get out of here. Take the laptop and your files, and work from home until she's better. However, I want you to check in every day with progress reports. No sitting around watching those soap operas or whatever daytime talk shows you ladies watch all day long. And get rid of ... *that*." He pointed to the wastebasket looking a bit green himself. "I have no use for it. Go!" He stood up with his hand covering his nose and mouth. From a drawer in his desk, he grabbed a can of Lysol and proceeded to spray every surface in his office as Tessa and Sophie left *with* the trashcan.

7

Tessa tucked Sophie back into bed and set herself up at her tiny kitchen table—laptop to her left, Shilling binder, adding machine, mechanical pencils, and all important Post-it notes to her right. Of course, her already filled, oversized coffee mug was front and center. Just as she was about to start working, the phone began to ring.

"Really?" she mumbled to herself. "He's probably just calling to check if he can hear a *soap opera or whatever daytime talk show us ladies watch all day long* in the background. Dumbass." She thought about turning the TV on just to mess with him, but then decided that would be a bad idea and quickly answered the phone instead. "Hello?"

"Um … hello," the male voice said.

Tessa pulled her phone back to look at the caller ID. It definitely wasn't Mr. Abbott. The man on the other end of the line sounded vaguely familiar, but the phone number wasn't at all recognizable.

"Can I help you?" she asked.

"Is this Tessa Haines?"

"Yes," she replied, still trying to place the voice.

"Oh, good, I do have the right number. The handwriting was a little messy, so I couldn't tell if this was a three or a five. But apparently it was a three after all."

"Who is this?" she asked. Game time was over.

"I'm sorry, I should have said right away. Forgive me. I'm coming off of a fifteen-hour shift. This is Brandon Hall … Dr. Hall. I treated your daughter in the emergency room last night."

So that's why his voice sounded familiar. "Yes, of course," she replied, trying to sound professional and not caught completely off guard. She paused for a minute, gathering herself. Just why was he calling her? Maybe one of Sophie's tests came back with bad news or something. Panic began to well in her chest.

"I was just calling to follow up."

"Follow up?" Tessa asked. So did that mean there was no bad news on test results? Was this normal hospital protocol? She didn't recall receiving follow up calls in the past. *There better not be a bill for this.*

"Yes, how is Sophie feeling today?"

Feeling a bit more relaxed, she took a sip of her coffee and leaned back in her chair. Maybe he could settle her nerves about Sophie's condition after the rough morning they had. "Well, her fever is lower, but she's not able to hold any food or liquid down, and she's coughing a lot. She's been sleeping off and on all morning. She just seems really uncomfortable and miserable."

"Poor thing," Dr. Hall replied. "If you'd like, I can take a look at her later."

"No rest for the weary, huh? They have you back at the hospital so soon after fifteen-hours there?"

"No, the hospital gives us a break now and again. I've got the coming two days off to rest up before my next marathon shift. I was thinking I could stop by … if you were worried about Sophie, I mean. I imagine it's hard having to take care of her on your own when she's so sick."

Tessa didn't know if she should be thankful for the offer or insulted. She prided herself on her ability to single parent Sophie, and while yes, she did ask her sisters for help more than she wanted, for the most part, she did okay on her own. Plus, did she really want to be with this guy alone in her apartment? Tessa had only been alone with a few men since Scott. After that debacle, she put up a wall—a fortress was more like it—and decided to devote her life to raising her daughter. None of the men since had been able to break through to her heart. Serious anxiety set in as she fanned herself with the papers sitting on her table.

"Miss Haines?" Dr. Hall asked. "Are you still there?"

"Yes, sorry," she replied. "I appreciate the offer, Dr. Hall, but I think it's probably best if I just let Sophie sleep it out today and see how she does. Like you said last night, we just have to let the virus work its way through her system."

"Most doctors don't do this, so I understand your hesitation. Let me give you my number in case you change your mind or if Sophie's condition worsens. Like I said, I don't have to go back to the hospital for forty-eight hours." He laughed. "I guess I'm not good at taking time off. Of course, if Sophie's condition does change, and you feel more comfortable going to the E.R., then by all means take her there, or call her pediatrician. The important thing is that she gets better."

Tessa took down his phone number. Maybe he really *was* just interested in Sophie. Was it possible he did this for all of his patients?

"Okay, thank you," she said, wondering if she was making the right decision to turn down an opportunity to have her daughter looked at again because of her own insecurities. "I appreciate your concern," she replied, saying good-bye and hanging up before she could change her mind.

For the third time in three hours, Tessa's phone rang.

"Again?" she muttered. She'd just gotten off the phone with her boss ten minutes ago. How did he expect her to work if he didn't leave her alone? She looked at the caller ID before answering and sighed in relief. *Holly.* Her sister must be on a lunch break.

"Hey, Hol." Standing up with the phone propped between her ear and her shoulder, Tessa walked over to examine the contents of her fridge. She might as well eat. It wasn't often she had the luxury of having a real meal for lunch.

"Hi. I haven't talked to you in days. Do you have a minute to gab, or will your boss skin your hide if he catches you not working every spare second of the day?"

"Actually, I'm working from home today," she responded, examining the date on the package of pre-chopped lettuce she'd bought last week. It expired two days ago. Tossing it in the trash bin, she sighed. The last thing she needed right now was food poisoning. Not that there was ever a good time for such a thing. She grabbed a container of yogurt instead. "Sophie's sick."

"*He* let you work from home? Was he drunk or something?"

Chuckling, she pulled a spoon out of the drawer. "No, disgusted." She told Holly the entire story, including the trip to the hospital and the ensuing phone call a few hours ago with Dr. Swoon-worthy.

"Wait a second," Holly said. "Let me get this straight. A gorgeous, eligible, rich *doctor* wanted to come over to sweep you off your feet, and you said *no thanks*?"

"First of all," she corrected, "we don't know that he's rich. I mean, he works at Crestmont Memorial. Isn't that where Jared worked? He didn't make a ton of money if I remember correctly."

Holly sighed. "Jared was on the maintenance crew. This guy's a doctor. I'm pretty sure they're not on the same pay scale."

"Second," Tessa continued, ignoring her sister's comment, "I didn't say he was gorgeous, I said he was *swoon-worthy*. There's a difference."

"Enlighten me."

"And third," she added, still ignoring her, "he offered to come check on *Sophie*, not sweep me off my feet. Isn't that all part of the Hippocratic Oath they take when they become doctors or something?"

"Newsflash, Tessa. I've *never* had a doctor call me after a visit, wanting to follow up with me *at my house*. I can bet Ava will say the same for her two kids. Sophie is three. Have *you* ever had a doctor offer to stop by for a check-up before?"

"No," she replied quietly. She knew Holly was right. Otherwise, she wouldn't have hesitated the way she had.

"Listen, I know you've been hurt—really hurt—but at some point you've got to let someone in. Don't you want to share your life with a partner? Don't you want Sophie to grow up with a father figure? I'm not saying this doctor is *the one*, but you'll never know if you don't give him a chance."

The tear rolled down her cheek faster than she could blink it away. Of course she wanted to share her life with someone special. She wanted to find the same magic her two older sisters had with their spouses. Ever since Scott left, she'd been so cautious. Was it possible to let someone in?

"You're right," she replied. "I'm ... scared, and I have Sophie to think about."

"That's okay, sweetie. You have every right to be scared, and you should of course take things slow with anyone you meet. I just think you shouldn't be so quick to judge everyone, that's all. I'm saying this out of love, okay? Lord knows I made some crappy decisions along the way. I'm so grateful I didn't marry Jared. If I had, I'd either be miserable or divorced by now. However, if I had let that bad experience close myself up to every future relationship, I would have never taken a chance on Ben. You're not that same spunky girl I used to know. Don't let someone from your past steal your spirit."

Nodding, even though Holly couldn't see her through the telephone, Tessa knew her sister was right. She wasn't the same girl. *That* girl would have yelled, "*Screw you, Scott*" from the rooftop and marched on with her head held high. Where *was* that girl?

8

"Yes, Mr. Abbott, I've emailed all of the reports as well as a detailed time sheet listing out which client items I've worked on since we last spoke." Tessa stretched her weary back as she looked at the clock on her microwave. It was nearly eight in the evening, and she'd finally managed to get Sophie down to sleep for the night, after a day of intermittent naps and Disney movies. Her boss had called five times during the day to check on her. Each time, she'd emailed him updates and time sheets as requested. Apparently, working from home meant she'd be available to work 24/7. It was time for her to be off the clock. "So, I'll check in with you in the morning then?" Holding her breath, she waited for her boss' reply. Her not so subtle announcement that the workday was potentially over was a bold move.

"Um … well … yes, yes, these reports seem to be in order. Call me first thing in the morning so we can go over your day's agenda." He abruptly hung up the telephone.

Pulling the receiver away from her ear, Tessa rolled her eyes. *Have a good evening, and thanks again for putting in a hard day of work that went way beyond your required eight hours.* Shaking her head, she logged off her computer and went to check on Sophie.

Her daughter looked peaceful in her usual curled up position with Daisy in one arm and Biddy in the other. As she walked into the room to give her a kiss, the pungent odor stopped her in her tracks. Sophie had thrown up in her sleep.

"Oh sweetie," she said, trying to get her to sit up. "We need to change you out of this nightie and get you clean."

Propping Sophie up, she felt the heat radiating from her forehead once again. *Shoot, her temperature was coming back.* She was barely awake as Tessa went to run a cool bath to help bring down the fever. By the time she returned, Sophie had gotten sick again and was crying. Tessa cleaned her up, wrapped her in a soft blanket, and carried her to the couch. Putting her reservations aside, she found the piece of paper with the doctor's number on it and began to call.

"Hello?" he answered.

"Hi. This is Tessa Haines. I'm sorry to call so late. It's about Sophie ... my daughter. You said I could call if she seemed worse."

"Yes, of course. I just need the address."

"When they're this young, they can get dehydrated so quickly," Dr. Hall said as he eased another dropper of fluids between Sophie's parched lips. "It's a vicious cycle. The fever leads to dehydration, the dehydration makes the fever worse. Of course, she has to be able to keep some fluids in her to have a fighting chance. I gave her something for her nausea, which should also help her sleep. In fact, I think you'll both be getting a better night's sleep." He looked up at Tessa with a gentle smile that made her heart flutter just a tiny bit.

"I really appreciate you coming out, Dr. Hall. I know you said it's not a problem, but it's late, and I'm sure you're exhausted, and it's your day off, and ... I'm sorry, I'm going to stop talking now."

He laughed quietly as they walked out of Sophie's room. "You don't have to stop talking, but you do need to stop calling me Dr. Hall. It's Brandon, and coming out here was my idea, remember? I wouldn't have offered if I didn't want to be here."

"Thanks. And that goes for me, too. The Dr. Hall part I mean. Well, for me it's Miss Haines." Shaking her head, she smiled and paused before speaking again. "What I'm trying to say is that you can call me Tessa."

"You got it, Tessa."

They stood awkwardly in Sophie's doorway, listening as she breathed deeply in her sleep.

"She sounds better already," she said, feeling so relieved that she made the right decision. Her daughter was definitely feeling better and was more comfortable. So was that it? Was he going to leave now?

"Well ... um," he said, looking around. "Would you mind terribly if I had something to drink?"

"Oh! I'm so sorry. How rude of me. Of course." She turned her back toward him to lead the way into the kitchen before the crimson red fully reached her cheeks.

Thankfully, he stopped at her sink to wash his hands, allowing her a moment to regroup before he faced her again. He glanced down to the towel he'd used to dry his hands and laughed. "I guess I should have asked first. Old habits die hard."

"No, it's fine," she said with a smile, as she opened her refrigerator. "I'm afraid I don't have much to offer. I've got soda that I opened about a year ago, but I'm sure it's probably flat, or I could make some coffee. I'm sorry. I usually just drink water, and I wasn't expecting company. I do also have Sophie's juice boxes.

They have Elmo on them. They're all the rage down at the daycare."

Brandon chuckled and looked around. "How about some wine?" he asked, motioning to the unopened bottle Tessa had on the counter.

She'd forgotten all about the bottle of red, sitting there, collecting dust. Ava had brought it over one night a couple of weeks ago, hoping to have a girls' night, but had to rush off in a hurry after receiving a distraught call from her babysitter before they'd had a chance to open it.

"Oh, um, sure," Tessa said, uncertain that was the response she really intended to give as she searched for a corkscrew.

She now had her answer. This was more than just a house call to check up on a sick patient. Taking a deep breath, she tried her best to keep her hands steady as she opened the bottle and poured two glasses. Holly's earlier words resonated in the back of her mind as she handed him his drink.

"Shall we sit?" he asked, looking around.

Scattered all over the kitchen table and chairs were papers—remnants from Tessa's workday that she hadn't had a chance to clean up. Amongst the papers was an empty bowl. The one she'd taken out for the dinner she never had a chance to prepare. She went straight from *work* to checking on Sophie to calling Dr. Hall … aka Dr. Swoon-worthy... aka Brandon. She probably shouldn't be drinking on an empty stomach, but didn't really have any appetizer type food to offer and felt awkward eating a bowl of cereal in front of the doctor with her glass of red wine.

"I was working from home today," she felt compelled to explain, looking at her mess. "Why don't we sit in the living room?"

The living room was more like a nook off of the kitchen where a loveseat, coffee table, and small television barely fit. She was forced to sit close to the doctor whether she wanted to or not.

"I know I keep thanking you," Tessa began, glad to have the wine glass to hold to keep her hands from fidgeting, "but I really am so grateful you make house calls. I've never seen Sophie so sick."

"It's my pleasure. I'm glad I was able to help her feel a little better," Brandon replied, looking straight at her.

She took a small sip of her wine, her mind filled with trepidation as she tried to convince herself to just relax.

"You have beautiful eyes," he added.

"Oh," she said, choking on her drink. "Sorry. You just caught me off guard there." She put her glass on the table and brought her hand up to her mouth, hoping no wine had dribbled out during her little coughing fit. *Relax, Tessa. They're not all Scott.* Bringing the corners of her lips up into a hint of a smile, she shyly said, "Let me try that again. Thank you."

Brandon put his glass on the table as well and reached over to touch Tessa's face. She'd always loved the feeling of a man's hand lightly caressing her cheek. It had been so long. Tracing the line of her chin and lips, he slowly drew her in closer until their lips finally met. She closed her eyes, letting herself enjoy the moment. Hands that started as soft strokes on her face, slowly made their way down to her neck, her back, to the tops of her thighs. One by one, she felt the blocks start to dissolve, and she pulled away slowly and smiled.

He gazed into her eyes as their foreheads touched. "Do you want to show me to your bedroom?" he whispered as he nibbled on her ear.

The words, acting as a trigger, instantly worked to rebuild the blocks, sealing them tightly. Her entire body stiffened as she pushed herself straight up to standing, ready to bolt into the kitchen for a sharp object if necessary.

"I–I think you should leave," she told him.

"I'm so sorry," he said, standing up as well. "I honestly don't know what came over me."

"You came over to check on my daughter ... I wasn't expecting ... this is wrong."

"I know," he said, looking down. "Again, I'm sorry. I truly did come over to check on your daughter. You're just ... so beautiful, and I was getting caught up in the moment. Really, I'm not usually like this. Please, you have to believe me."

"We don't even know each other," she said.

"You're right. Please tell me you'll give me a second chance. I'd really like an opportunity to start over. Would you like to go out to dinner with me, on a proper date? After Sophie is better, of course. We could just talk."

Studying his eyes, she tried to figure out if he was sincere or feeding her some line. One thing she knew for sure was that this evening was now over. She walked to the front door to let him know it was time to leave. He followed her, looking like a child who'd just been scolded.

Turning around before walking into the hallway, he added one final plea, "Just one dinner. I promise to make it up to you."

Oh, what the hell, she thought, somewhat amused by his reaction. Hadn't Ava misjudged Max at first also? She smiled and replied, "I suppose that would be okay. And thanks for coming to check on Sophie."

9

"Go ahead," Holly began before taking another bite of her pizza, "say it."

"Say what? What am I missing?" Ava asked, looking around Tessa's small kitchen table at her younger sisters. Reaching for the salad bowl, she helped herself to a generous portion and passed it around.

Tessa loved nights like this—hanging out with Ava and Holly for a casual girls' only dinner. This time, Ava's husband was home with her kids. There would be no emergency phone call from any babysitters requiring her to end the evening early. Sophie was in the living room watching cartoons, snuggled on the couch with Daisy and Biddy. Her giggles filtered through to the kitchen, a sure sign she was on the mend. Four days had passed since the doctor's visit. She seemed almost completely recovered and had been fever free for just over twenty-four hours. Tessa was set to return to her office on Monday.

"Tessa met someone," Holly blurted, unable to contain her excitement. "A doctor. A *hot* doctor. Now I'm just waiting for her to say, '*You were right, Holly. I needed to loosen up and let someone in*'." She looked at her sister with a furrowed brow. "You haven't told Ava yet about your new *friend?*"

Getting up to grab a napkin, Tessa leaned against the sink, facing her sisters. In all honesty, at times Ava could be difficult to talk to about these sorts of things, especially with their age difference of six years. Sometimes Tessa felt like she was talking to her mom rather than her sister, and in return, Ava often gave lectures rather than advice. It hadn't always been that way. She guessed it started when Sophie was born. Maybe Tessa felt a bit insecure around her older sister, who was the perfect wife and mother, raising her children in the ideal nuclear family, the way it was *supposed* to be done. A lot of things changed about Tessa when Sophie was born, or maybe they changed before that, when Scott left her. *Don't let someone from your past steal your spirit.* She couldn't get Holly's words from the other day out of her head. That's exactly what happened, wasn't it?

"So?" Ava asked, staring at her sister with a curious smile. "Are you going to fill me in or what?"

"There's not much to tell. Sophie got sick. I brought her to the emergency room. The doctor who treated her was kind of good looking. Then he kissed me and—"

"Wait a minute!" Ava held up her hand to stop Tessa from talking. "You kissed in the hospital?"

"No," she laughed. "That would be weird … and highly inappropriate." She filled her oldest sister in on the home visit that turned into a … what exactly did it turn into? It definitely wasn't a date, and she still wasn't sure she trusted his intentions. Was his plan all along just to come over to see how far he could get? Shaking her head slightly to get her doubts out of her head, she continued her story. "We kissed for a little bit, which was nice, but then he went from Dr. Swoon-worthy to Dr. Want-to-get-in-my-pants in record time. I felt like I was back in high school necking with some boy on the couch. I kept waiting for Dad to barge in the room. Which, in this situation, actually would have been okay."

"Except, he's not just some high school boy," Holly reminded her. "He's a well-established and highly respected emergency room doctor who heads up the pediatrics department at Crestmont Memorial."

Tessa stared at her. "And how would you know that, Hol? What did you do, look him up on the Internet or something?"

"What? My fifth graders are all busy with district testing this week. I have to fill my time doing something at school. Unfortunately, I couldn't find out anything about his personal life, but I did find out he graduated Magna Cum Laude from UPenn Medical School. That's one of the Ivy Leagues, you know, and tops in pediatrics, too. He's without a doubt daddy material."

"Are you serious?" Tessa asked, rolling her eyes. "Just because he takes care of sick kids, doesn't mean he wants some of his own. And it certainly doesn't mean he wants to be a dad to a kid who's not even his. Maybe he likes going home to a childless house. Who wants to take their work home anyway?"

"Um, I do, remember? I love kids," Holly stated, her voice suddenly changing from her usual perky self to somber. "I'd kill to go home to a house full of children every night."

Tessa looked over at her. Was that a tear forming in her eye? Were her and Ben having trouble getting pregnant? She'd just assumed they'd put off their plans for a while. It never occurred to her there were any problems.

"Hol? Are you okay?" she asked.

With her hands, she brushed Tessa off dismissively, letting her know there would be no discussion, as Ava put her arm around her shoulder to comfort her. Yes, there was definitely something going on there she knew nothing about.

"So," her oldest sister stated, "what happened after the good doctor turned into a raging hormonal teenage boy?"

Holly snorted. Ava always seemed to know exactly what to say to bring everyone out of their funks. Maybe Tessa really could talk to her about matters of the heart.

"I put the brakes on. I mean, we don't even know anything about each other. Hell, Holly apparently knows more about him than I do at this point."

Holly nodded and shrugged her shoulders.

"And? Is anything going on with you and this mystery doctor now?" Ava asked, raising her eyebrows.

"I'm not sure," Tessa said. "He apologized and begged me to let him take me to dinner. On a real date—sort of a do-over, I guess—so we can talk and get to know each other before he turns into an octopus again. I agreed, and now I haven't talked to him since. He was here four nights ago, and said he had another marathon shift coming up. I'm guessing he'll call once he catches up on some sleep, or maybe I scared him away."

"I doubt it," Ava said. "He knows you want to take things slow. Sounds like he's just respecting your wishes."

"I suppose. Still, a call or a text to check in would be okay. Men can be so literal sometimes."

"And dumb," Holly added.

"You see? This is why I stopped dating. I don't want to be that girl who sits around analyzing a guy's every move. *Is he going to call? When is he going to call? If he calls too soon, he just wants sex. If he waits too long, he doesn't like me. If he only texts, he's taking the easy way out. If he doesn't text, he doesn't care.* Without a guy in my life it's just me and Sophie, and we're all good."

"Who says you have to be *that* girl? She isn't the confident, independent Tessa Haines we know. The girl we know would sit here and say, *'That doctor was kind of hot but got out of hand, so I put him in his place and made him beg for a second chance'.*"

"That's what I did."

"Exactly," Holly reminded her. "Because you're not that needy, emotional girl you described."

"That's true, but on the other hand ..."

"What?"

"It was nice to be wrapped up in someone's arms. Someone other than my sisters', I mean."

"Someone *swoon-worthy?*" Holly teased.

Tessa's lips curled into a smile and she nodded. "Someone swoon-worthy."

10

"So, you decided to come back to work finally, huh? Well, I hope you enjoyed your little vacation."

Mr. Abbott wasted no time calling Tessa into his office first thing Monday morning. He sat behind his desk, drinking black coffee that smelled like the burnt sludge from the bottom of the pot that had sat for hours on end. It probably had been sitting there all week actually, since she was the only one who ever cleaned out that darned thing. *A woman's job* was no doubt what he thought. He took another sip and had a smug look on his face, his beady eyes never blinking as he stared her down.

Was he trying to be funny? No. Her boss didn't do funny. He was all business, all the time. Focusing on the gold plated pen and pencil set that sat perched at the edge of his desk, she tried to think of an appropriate response so as not to lose her temper. Last week was neither restful nor relaxing. She worked sixteen-hour days, took care of a sick child, catered to a needy, arrogant boss, and barely ate or slept. She was pretty sure there was no vacation involved.

"You told me it was okay to work at home while my daughter had the flu, sir. I was working the entire time and actually put in more hours than I normally do when I'm here. I checked in with you several times a day and sent you detailed time sheets and reports. You seemed okay with it all at the time. It was your idea, don't you remember?"

He stared at her, sitting completely still; not speaking, or moving ... not even blinking. He was alive, wasn't he? Yes, he did appear to be breathing. Was he waiting for her to say something else?

"Well," she stumbled, "the doctor said her virus could last up to two weeks, and my daughter was much better in less than a week, so I guess we got lucky."

The doctor. His shift was long over by now, and he still hadn't called. However, there was no time to dwell on him. At the moment, she needed to brace herself for what appeared to be an unexpected attack from her schizophrenic boss.

Mr. Abbott put his coffee cup down and tapped his fingers together, but still said nothing. At least he was moving now. Looking around his office, Tessa nervously waited for his response. There were no family photos, plants, works of art, or other items normally found in the offices of professionals. The only items displayed on his dark paneled walls were enormous frames exhibiting his multiple diplomas and certificates flaunting all of his accolades. Sitting in the middle of the office was his oversized leather-topped mahogany desk with matching hammered nail-head daunting leather chairs for his clients, one of which she sat in. He had an executive-style chair for himself that looked more like a king's throne. There was a bar set up in the corner with several decanters filled with what she assumed were various liquors. All in all, the office seemed like a perfect set up for an intimidating narcissist, like himself.

"Lucky is not the word that comes to mind," he finally responded, handing her a stack of papers from across his desk. "These are the reports you did for Mr. Schilling while you were at home ... *working*. You were going off of his old numbers and guessing. These will mean nothing to him. Monkeys could have done that and possibly better. These were a complete waste of your time ... and mine."

Taking the reports, she did her best not to roll her eyes. It wasn't easy. He knew she only had old numbers to work off of when he insisted she re-do them all. She even tried to explain that to him. He purposely set her up to fail. *Again.*

"Nicholas is in London right now. Call over to his office, and see when his new broker and bank statements will be available. I told him we'd have some interim reports ready instead since we missed this past quarter's meeting. I'll need some preliminary projections right away. And they'll need to be perfect. Then we'll have to do a full work-up for next quarter. There is no room for error here. Do you think you can handle that, or shall I put a call in to the Forest Hills Zoo for a replacement?"

Tessa glared at Mr. Abbott. With Sophie being sick all week, and her boss appearing to act somewhat human—what with letting her work from home and all—she'd forgotten to scour the want ads for a new job. Stupid her for thinking he might actually be growing a heart.

"I can handle it," she snapped.

"Good." Getting up from his desk, he grabbed his keys and his briefcase. "I've got client meetings the rest of the day. I trust I can leave you alone to work."

This time she did roll her eyes … directly at him. *Was he serious?* She didn't care if he was her boss. She'd had enough of the *sirs* and other usual niceties. Turning on her heels, she walked straight out of his office. Her heart was beating so loud she could barely hear herself think. Let him fire her. She was fed up with his crap. She sat at her desk, turned on her computer with trembling hands, and waited for the repercussions of her blatant disrespect.

After several minutes, there was a knock on the doorframe of her office. Holding her breath, she refused to look up from her computer screen.

"I'm leaving now, Tessa. I'll have my cell if there is anything urgent, although I have no doubt you're more than capable of handling things. I'll see you tomorrow. Have a good day."

She opened her eyes wide, still staring straight ahead. "Thank you, sir," she said, turning her head slowly toward him. "You have a good day as well. I'm sure everything will be fine here."

Bringing her head back to her computer, she smiled. Maybe she needed to stand up for herself more often to gain some respect. First the doctor, now her boss. Yes, some of that spirit Holly was talking about was indeed starting to resurface after all. She waited until she saw Mr. Abbott's car leave the parking lot and picked up the phone to call Mr. Schilling's office.

11

"**G**ood morning, Nicholas Schilling Capital Ventures. How may I direct your call?"

Tessa twirled the pencil in her hands. Even the receptionist sounded pretentious, or maybe she was just happy. At the very least she was well paid. With the generous Christmas bonus that woman received, she made almost twice the salary Tessa did this past year, just for answering phones. Of course Tessa noticed ... she received copies of Shilling's bank statements every month. It was hard not to notice checks with that many zeros on them.

Mr. Abbott's idea of a Christmas bonus was letting her leave at four-thirty on Christmas Eve instead of five. She wondered if Schilling's office was hiring. Wouldn't that be a kicker?

"Mr. Abbott? I quit. Oh yeah, I'm going to work for Nicholas Schilling. But don't worry, I'll put in a good word for you. I'm sure after I'm done telling him what a stellar member of society you truly are, he'll gladly keep you on as his personal accountant and financial manager." She smiled as she tried to picture his face contorting when she told him the news. Or maybe it would be more fun to have Abbott and Associates remain on as Schillings' accountant. Stretching her feet out, she imagined what it would be like working for the other side: *"Steven, we'll need those reports to be done first thing Monday morning and without error. Do you think you can handle that, or should we put in a call to the Forest Hills Zoo?"* She giggled silently to herself just thinking about it.

"Hello?" the voice asked. "Is there anybody there?"

"Oh," she said, straightening back up. "I'm so sorry. Yes, this is Tessa Haines calling from Abbott and Associates. Can you connect me to Mr. Schilling's assistant please?"

"Certainly. One moment."

She scrolled through the texts and emails on her cell while the bland music played on the line as she waited. Still nothing from the doctor.

"Nicholas Schilling's office," the unfamiliar female voice said. Usually when she called, she dealt with Greta, his administrative assistant. They'd never met, but they'd been speaking to each other on the phone for as long as her boss had been their client.

"Hello," Tessa began, "is Greta available?" She knew she could probably ask the person who answered the phone for the statements, but then she'd have to explain who she was, who she worked for, and why she needed to see Mr. Schilling's bank and brokerage statements. She doubted someone would just hand over that type of information without giving her the third-degree. At least she hoped they wouldn't. Speaking directly with his assistant would be much easier.

"No, I'm sorry," the frazzled voice said, "Greta is out on personal leave. I'm with the temp agency, filling in until she comes back. At least, we think she's coming back. Can I help you with something?"

Huh, perhaps there might be an opening in that office soon after all. Tessa laughed silently and shook her head. No, Schilling was probably way more demanding than her own boss. The temps exhausted voice alone seemed to prove that.

"I'm calling from Abbott and Associates. We're Mr. Schilling's personal accountants. My name is Tessa Haines and—"

"Yes," the woman said, abruptly interrupting her. Apparently time she had no time to waste on the telephone. "There's a note here that you'd be calling. Mr. Schilling wanted me to let you know he's contacted all of his banks, and they expect to have his statements ready in a few days. He'll have his financial assistant drop them off at your office early next week."

"Oh," she replied, surprised. That went a lot easier than she was expecting. "Great, thank you very much."

Hanging up the phone, she was relieved to have accomplished the most important task on Mr. Abbott's list. Now there really was nothing left to work on for Schilling today, other than clearing out all the old numbers to get the reports prepped for the new information. After that, she could tackle the growing pile of work for the other clients. Those poor *other* clients ... they always took the back burner.

"So what do you think, Hol? It's been a week. Should I call him?"

Tessa kept one eye on the parking lot as she talked to her sister. With her luck, Mr. Abbott would pull in and catch her on a personal call during her lunch break. *A break? How absurd.*

"Why not? It can't hurt. With the schedule he keeps, he's probably lost track of time. You could always make the excuse that you just wanted to let him know Sophie was doing much better or something."

"Oh great," Tessa said, taking a bite of her sandwich. For once, she remembered to pack real food and actually had time to sit back and eat it. "Now I'm using my daughter as a pawn to get men?"

"Only the hot ones," Holly teased.

"I don't know. Something doesn't feel right to me. I can't explain it."

"I can. It's called fear, and it's never going to go away if you don't push through it. I thought we'd been over this. Anyway, I hate to cut this short, but I've got to go convince a bunch of fifth graders they will indeed use long division again at some point in their lives. I'll talk to you later. Don't work too hard, and *call him.* Love you."

"Love you, too, Hol—" Tessa started to say, but her sister had already hung up. *Fear ... right.* She shook her head, attempting to rid herself of the feeling. *Why not?* With her cell phone still in her hand, she dialed before she lost her nerve. It went straight to voicemail. "Hi ... Brandon. This is Tessa. Tessa Haines. I was calling to say hi. Well, and to thank you again for coming over to check on Sophie. She's made a full recovery and is back at daycare. Um, anyway, I, uh, wasn't sure of your schedule, but I know you had mentioned getting together again. And, well, I'm back at work, but it's only during the day, so I'm free in the evenings ... or on the weekends. Whatever works for your schedule is fine. I'm flexible. Just let me know. Okay. So ... I guess I'll talk to you soon. Thanks. Bye."

Shit. She threw her phone into her purse and shook it down to the bottom. Could she have possibly sounded anymore desperate? Putting her head down on her desk, she tried to will the powers that be to turn back time—just three minutes would do to erase that call. She could hear her phone buzzing from inside her bag. *Ugh.* Why did she bury it? What if it was Sophie's daycare? She dug through and grabbed it in time to see she'd worried for nothing.

"Ava, hi." Tessa felt flustered, yet relieved to hear her sister's voice. After leaving that message, she was no longer in a hurry to talk to Brandon.

"Hey, are you busy?"

"No, I'm on my lunch break. How's everything?"

"Everything is fine. Max is already off again on another flight. It's international this time, and then he's got others lined up, so he'll be gone until Sunday."

She could hear the sadness in her sister's voice. It had to be so hard on her and the kids having him gone so much.

"Do you need some help?" It was time for her to return some of the favors she'd burdened Ava with lately. "I can take Logan and Jenna for a few hours this weekend if you need to get some things done. I'm sure Sophie would love the company."

"Thanks," Ava replied, "but what I really need is a date."

"Excuse me?"

"Let me rephrase that," she started to explain. "I received an invitation to a gallery exhibit for this Friday night. It's been so long since I've been to an event like this. I'd really love to go, but I hate to go to these things solo."

"So you want me to find you a date?" Tessa asked, confused. "I don't know, Av. I can't even find myself a date. Does Max know about this?"

Ava laughed. "No, silly. I want *you* to be my date. I've already arranged for a babysitter. You can bring Sophie to my house. She can even sleep over if she wants. You both can. What do you say? It's a chance to get all fancied up for the night. It'll be fun. Promise. They'll have free food and drinks …"

"Well, when you put it like that. It sounds great. Thanks."

12

It was almost time to leave for the day, and Tessa was in the middle of compiling reports for a client, when her cell phone started to ring. She was so wrapped up in her work that she nearly missed the call.

"Hello, hello?" she said into the phone, hoping she'd grabbed it in time before the person on the other end was sent to her voicemail. She hadn't recognized the number off hand and hoped it wasn't Sophie's daycare or Mr. Abbott calling from a client's office.

"Hi Tessa. It's Brandon."

Startled by the sound of his voice, her heart instantly began beating faster. She put her file to the side and tried to calm herself. "Brandon ... hi. How are you?"

"I'm good," he replied. "I'm sorry I haven't had a chance to call. That flu really took its toll on the staff at the hospital, and I've been pulling double shifts to cover for sick doctors. I've barely been back to my house since I saw you and haven't had a moment to myself to do much of anything."

"Wow, that's awful," she told him, now feeling bad she'd bothered him with her desperate sounding phone call.

"Yes, but we're finally starting to get back to normal. I got your message, and I'm so glad to hear Sophie's doing better. I was hoping you'd get in touch with me to let me know how she was ... and to let me know how you were doing, as well."

Feeling her cheeks starting to flush, Tessa tried to think of something interesting and witty to say. "I'm doing okay. I'm back to my regular work schedule. You know, getting paid pennies to count other people's millions." *Crap.* Now she sounded desperate *and* poor.

"So, I promised you a dinner if I remember correctly. Are you free Saturday night?"

"I am," she replied, feeling tinges of fear creeping back in.

"Great. How about I pick you up at seven?"

She'd never hear the end of it from her sisters if she said no and already knew Holly would watch Sophie for her since all of this was her idea. "Seven is good."

"I'll see you then. I'm looking forward to it, Tessa," he said in his swoon-worthy voice that both made her heart melt and bring forward her insecurities all in the same breath.

The line went dead before she was able to respond.

"Tell me again how Dr. Steam-worthy looked into your eyes and instantly cured Sophie?" Ben mocked while helping himself to a third helping of Holly's lasagna.

Tessa and Sophie had stopped over to their place for dinner. It used to be a regular Wednesday night thing, but with school conferences and Sophie getting sick, it had been a while since they'd all seen each other.

Holly playfully swatted her husband across his head with her napkin. "It's swoon-worthy, not steam-worthy, and he didn't cure Sophie by staring into Tessa's eyes. He's an emergency room doctor, not some quack magician."

Tessa shook her head and smiled before taking another bite of her dinner. She so adored Ben. He was like the big brother she never had. Of course she loved Max, too, but she never really had a chance to get to know him. She was only sixteen when he and Ava got engaged and moved across the country. Now that they were back here in Forest Hills, Max was hardly ever home because of his job as an airline pilot. They just didn't hang out much, or at least not the way she hung out with Ben. They'd been close since before he and Holly even started dating. In fact, she was the one Ben relentlessly texted to get advice about her sister. Their relationship was special. Maybe it was because he was just a big goof … constantly in a good mood and always interested in what was going on in her life.

"Come on, Ben. It wasn't so long ago you gave Holly the same look. You know what I'm talking about. I saw it at Ava's wedding. You even kept it up after she kicked your ass playing pool. Just out of curiosity, have you won a game yet, Benny boy?"

Glancing at his wife, he scowled. "She refuses to play me anymore."

Tessa started laughing and looked over to her sister. "Hol? Is this true?"

"Yup. That's right. I cut him off after he accused me of cheating. Can you believe that? I ask you, who in their right mind would call their own wife a cheater? I'll tell you who, someone afraid to admit that they suck at pool, that's who."

Tessa dramatically drew in her breath. "Benjamin Oakes! How could you?"

"Now hold on a minute," he began, holding his hands up to stop the onslaught from the sisters. Having one sister on his case was bad enough, but having two gang up on him at the same time was something Tessa imagined he wanted to avoid at all costs. "I never called Holly a cheater. I only made a comment that I found it *interesting* that she's gone so many years now without losing, that's all. Some may have taken that as a compliment. I personally find it fascinating she got defensive over it. However, for the record, *never* did I use the word cheater. Am I right, oh lovely wife whom I adore with all of my heart and soul?"

Putting her arms around her husband's neck, Holly nuzzled her face into Ben's hair. "It's okay, babe. You do what you have to do to make yourself feel better. We all understand. I know it can't be easy to have your wife beat you at pool ... what, like about five hundred times now?"

He rolled his eyes and smirked. "How did we get on this subject anyway? I thought we were talking about Tessa and her new boyfriend, Dr. Spark-worthy."

"Swoon-worthy!" Tessa and Holly both corrected before breaking out into a fit of laughter.

"And he's not my boyfriend. We've only been on one date ... not even a date, really. It was more like a house call."

Ben opened his mouth to make a comment, but Holly quickly put her hand over it before he could get the lewd, sarcastic words out.

Tessa raised her eyebrows and shook her head. "What is it with you men? Pigs, all of you. The house call was for Sophie."

"Aw, come on, Tessa. You set me up for that one," he responded, making sad puppy dog eyes.

She laughed. "Yeah, the good doctor made that look, too, when I shut him down."

"Shut him down? Ugh. That's just cruel. I'm surprised he's agreed to see you again," he remarked.

"She's a Haines," Holly interjected. "Of course he wants to see her again. Don't listen to him, Tessa. Brandon will wait until you're good and ready."

"You know I'm just teasing, right?" Ben asked, suddenly changing to a more serious tone. "Holly knows what she's talking about. If he doesn't wait until you're ready, he's not the guy for you. Lord knows your sister made me wait," he grumbled, looking at his wife. "A man's got needs you know."

Holly swatted him with her napkin again. "A man's got two hands, and I was worth the wait. So is Tessa."

"She's right," he said, looking at his sister-in-law. "You deserve his respect and so much more. Don't ever doubt that."

Tessa nodded. She hoped Holly realized just how lucky she was. "Don't worry," she said. "He knows what the deal is ... dinner, that's all. If he tries that fast hands crap again, I'll really show him what *shut him down* means."

Her sister sighed with a concerned look. "Just try to have a good time, okay?"

13

"You look beautiful." Ava put another safety pin into the back of the dress Tessa had borrowed for the gallery event that evening. She hadn't worn a dress this fancy since Holly's wedding three years ago. "It's too bad that doctor can't see you in this. Maybe you can wear it again on your date tomorrow night."

"I doubt we're going somewhere requiring me to wear anything this swanky ... but I do look hot," she agreed, admiring her reflection in the mirror. Deep purple always was a good color on her, complementing her dark brown hair and blue eyes, and accentuating her flawless porcelain skin.

While twisting her body to get a better look would probably be the most lady-like thing to do in this situation, it was just not going to cut it. Instead, she stood on her toes and twirled—*twice*. It was the only proper way to fully appreciate the ensemble. She was so sick of wearing business attire every day. Her wardrobe was so pathetic: conservative suits and ill-fitting comfort clothes. It was no wonder she felt so down on herself most of the time. She twirled around a third time.

"Watch those sudden moves. You don't want these pins to pop." Ava watched her sister in the mirror and smiled. "You do look hot, though. Just how did you manage to give birth and still keep your hips so tiny? I should hate you, you know."

Turning around, Tessa looked at her sister. Ava looked fabulous in a Kelly green velvet dress. Her long, auburn hair cascaded over her shoulders, and her hazel eyes sparkled with flecks of green that matched the gorgeous fabric she wore. Of course, Ava would look spectacular in a potato sack.

"What are you talking about? You're stunning. You always have been." It's true. Ava was always known as the gorgeous one when referring to the Haines sisters. She was tall and elegant—a natural beauty—while Tessa was often referred to as the cutest of the three. A bubbly, cheerleader type, she had a slender frame, long brown hair with perfect natural waves, a little button nose, bright blue eyes, and an engaging smile that could light up a room—when she smiled that was. Holly, the only blonde in the family, had more of a wholesome girl next-door look to her with warm brown eyes and freckles.

"It feels odd to wear something without stains on it," Ava teased, examining the front of her dress as if she were double-checking. "I'm just glad I never got rid of these clothes from my old life in the art world."

Tessa watched her sister's expression, examining it for sadness or regret. "Do you miss it? The excitement of having a career in something you were once so passionate about?"

"Sometimes, but I'm doing something else I'm really passionate about right now, and it's even more fulfilling."

"Mom!" Jenna yelled from downstairs as if on cue. "Logan just spilled all of his juice on his new pajamas!"

Shaking her head, she let out a breathy sigh. "At least most of the time it is. I'm thinking I may need to add in more nights like tonight, though, so I get to do both."

"Don't worry, Mrs. Haines!" the babysitter yelled. "I've got it!"

"Come on, we'd better get going before the babysitter changes her mind and bolts. The art world awaits!"

Walking through the front doors of the gallery, Tessa was instantly captivated. Unlike her older sister, she'd never been to an event like this before. In fact, she was embarrassed to admit she'd never even been to an art gallery. Opening nights at the university and community theaters where she'd worked were really the only openings she was used to. Those types of events were completely different. Dressing up meant wearing your good jeans. Pizza and beer were the norm, with maybe a bottle of cheap champagne to spray over the cast and crew afterwards to celebrate. Here, people were in formal gowns and tuxedos, sipping what she assumed was not so cheap champagne. There was no pizza to be found; instead, fancy appetizers were passed around on silver trays by men and women wearing white gloves. At theater openings there were bear hugs and slaps on the back. Here there were fake air kisses on cheeks and formal handshakes. Guests tonight acted as if they were in a library rather than at a party, talking in hushed tones as they mulled about looking at paintings tagged with numbers priced with many, *many* zeros after the dollar signs. Did Ava really enjoy hanging out with these pretentious snobs?

"You're not here to buy something, are you?" Tessa asked, unable to take her eyes off the prices. She knew Max made a decent salary, but she didn't think he made *that* much. One of these paintings could pay a year's worth of her rent, including utilities, and possibly gas and groceries as well.

Ava laughed. "No, I've just always loved this artist, Claudette Rayne. She held several exhibits at the gallery I ran in California. I haven't seen her in years. There she is. Come, let me introduce you."

Barely able to keep her balance on her heels, Tessa accidentally bumped into a woman as her sister grabbed her hand and hurried her across the room.

"I'm so sorry," she said, tugging away from Ava in order to stop to apologize.

"It's no problem," the woman responded, smiling kindly.

"Here's your drink, darl—"

That voice. Watching the man as he approached the woman, Tessa was unable to speak. She shut her eyes for a split second, thinking she had to be seeing things, and opened them back up. Nope, there was no mistake. *Was he about to call this woman darling?*

"Tessa?" Ava asked, now standing by her side. "Are you okay?"

Tessa slowly took her eyes off the man and looked at her sister, forcing the corners of her mouth into a tiny smile.

"Ava," she began, "this is Dr. Hall. He's the doctor who treated Sophie in the hospital recently when she had the flu. *Remember?*" She brought her eyes back to him and squinted, trying to get a read on him, but his expression remained blank. *So he was out with someone. Big deal. It's not like they were a couple or anything.* "Dr. Hall, it's nice to see you again. This is my sister, Ava. "

"Oh," Ava murmured, looking at Tessa rather than the doctor. She waited for Tessa to nod to her—a sign to follow her lead. "It's … nice to meet you, Dr. Hall. Thank you for taking such good care of my niece."

"It was my pleasure," he replied, matter-of-factly.

"I'm sorry," Tessa said, addressing the woman and trying to maintain a friendly tone to her voice, "how rude of me. I'm Tessa Haines." She held out her hand.

"Nice to meet you," she said, seemingly oblivious to the tension churning amongst them. "I'm Jeannie Hall, Dr. Hall's wife."

Tessa kept her smile, trying not to show any reaction as her brain screamed, *Wife?* Now it was a big deal. *What the hell?* For a split second, she thought about causing a scene, but decided he really wasn't worth it. She felt sorry for the woman, actually. That asshole probably hit on every decent looking woman that walked through the E.R., and she couldn't help wondering how many of them fell for his tricks. She was proud of herself for not sleeping with him that night. Of course, it also proved Holly wasn't right at all. It wasn't fear she had felt, it was intuition, and she should have listened to it the first time.

"Well, then. It's nice to meet you, Jeannie. And I'm sorry again for bumping into you. Have fun tonight," she said in a remarkably calm voice. She moved her eyes slowly back over to Brandon for a brief, yet strong and deliberate glare. She wouldn't be looking at or speaking to him ever again.

14

"More."

"I think you've had enough, Tessa."
Ava pulled the pitcher out of her hand mid-pour,
placing it down on the table.

After the run in with Dr. Sleazy at the gallery, Ava
said a quick hello to the artist she came to see, made a
round of even quicker good-byes, and led Tessa
straight out the door and over to Holly's house. They
were still dressed in their formal attire as they sat
around her kitchen table for an impromptu girls' night
gathering.

"What are you talking about?" Tessa asked, taking
it back and filling her glass. She gulped down the

contents in one swoop. "Holly makes a kickass vanilla milkshake, and I'm starving. You made us leave before I could eat any of that fancy grub." Licking the white ice cream mustache off the top of her lips, she added, "Got any snacks to go with this?"

"It is a shame we left so soon," Ava agreed. "The food at those things are always one of the highlights. I just figured you'd want to get out of there."

Tessa shrugged. "Maybe, although it's probably best we left when we did. There was a chance Dr. Gigolo might have met Ms. Fist if we stayed any longer." She turned abruptly to face her other sister. "You see, Holly? This is why I didn't want to call him. *'Call him, Tessa. He's just respecting your wishes to go slow. Face your fears. Don't you want a father figure for Sophie?'*" Licking the inside of her glass, she tried to get every last drop of ice cream out. "You know," she continued, "I should have gone with my gut. I *knew* something was off with him. My gut never lies. *My gut* told me Sophie and I were just fine living comfortably on our own."

"You mean living locked up in the fortress you built around you that no one can penetrate," Holly corrected, filling a bowl with pretzels.

"At least one good thing came out of this night," Tessa told her sisters. "The good 'ole doc got to see me in this gorgeous dress after all. Isn't that what you said before we left, Ava? *Too bad you can't wear that on your date with him tomorrow?* Looks like your wish came true ... sort of. It wasn't a date, and it's not tomorrow night, but he did get to see me looking *mighty fine.*" She picked up her now empty glass and began twirling it around to catch her reflection. Yup, Cinderella went to the ball all right, except before her coach could turn into a pumpkin, her prince turned into a rat.

Ava pursed her lips together and took the cup away from her before it broke. "It's not entirely what I intended, but ... well ..." A tiny laugh escaped her lips. "You did walk away looking damn good that's for sure. I still can't believe he's married. I don't think any of us saw that coming. How could we?"

"Seriously," Holly said, sitting back down as she placed the snacks on the table. "I admit it, I was way off base with this guy. I mean ... shit, *married?* Major asshole."

"Serious major asshole," Ben interjected, walking in the room. "Sorry, I didn't mean to interrupt. I know it's your sacred girl time and all. I just couldn't help but overhear some of that. You ladies are being kind of loud. No offense." Putting an arm around Tessa's shoulders, he leaned in close. "Don't forget what I told you the other day. You deserve the best, and this guy is far from it. He's the sludge they scrape off of the machine parts down at the plant at the end of the day. You want me to send some of my guys over to the hospital parking lot after his shift ends to mess with him?"

"Are you a thug leader now?" Holly asked, smirking.

He stood back up and swiped a handful of pretzels out of the bowl before hopping up on the counter. "No, I just don't like seeing Tessa get screwed over. She's like my little sister."

"Thanks, but I think I'll pass," Tessa noted. "Besides, he's just going to keep doing this whether you mess up his pretty face or not. He'll wait for the next single, unsuspecting girl to walk through his exam room, act like he gives a damn about her kid, and make his move. You think he cares about me, or the next girl, or the one after that? He's only interested in one thing."

"What a scumbag," Ava said, shaking her head.

"That's Dr. Scumbag," Holly added, snickering.

"Anyway," her oldest sister continued, "you handled yourself amazingly; with dignity and class ... and daggers." She looked up at Ben. "You should have seen the look she gave him. It was priceless. Right in front of his wife, too. Very subtle, but strong. I would have been a blubbering mess if it were me." She reached across the table for Tessa's hands and gave them a squeeze.

"Guys like that aren't worth crying over," Tessa stated, smiling at her sister. "In fact, the older I get, the more I realize most guys aren't worth crying over at all. I suppose that will be the telltale sign for me. If he's worth my tears, he's a keeper. Now there's a depressing personal ad. *Single, white female looking for man who can make me cry.*"

"You've got it all wrong, Tessa," Ben said, jumping down to walk over to the table. "Take it from a male perspective. Then I'm leaving the room. I know I'm not supposed to be in here, but just listen. Not all guys are like that jerk. Really. Most of us are only insecure buffoons. We don't know squat about women. We don't know how to act, or even talk to a woman when we meet someone we like, and nine times out of ten, we're going to make you cry. But most of the time, it's not on purpose. Usually, it's because we're stupid creatures who don't know any better. All we want is a chance to prove we're actually decent humans who have big hearts."

"See that?" Tessa said, feeling her eyes well up. "He's making me cry. Can we clone him, Holly?"

"Nope," she replied, wrapping her arms around her husband's waist, "but don't worry. I have a really good feeling that one day you'll find your own stupid buffoon. Now you," she said, pushing her husband away with a smile, "go. You've taken up enough of our time. Don't you have some sort of manly sports thing to watch on television?"

"Yes, and while I'm at it," he stated, grabbing a beer out of the refrigerator, "I think I'll see if I can burp out the alphabet during the commercials." Ben mouthed the word *buffoon* as he slowly walked backward out of the room.

"He must keep you laughing all day long," Ava told her, chuckling.

Holly nodded. "He's a good guy. So is Max, and somewhere out there is the perfect guy for Tessa."

"Agreed," Ava stated. "Who wouldn't want you? And Sophie. You both are amazing. You just have to be patient, and you have to be willing to give someone a chance." She pointed to her heart as a symbol of where Tessa kept her walls.

Rolling her eyes, she shook her head. Her sisters meant well, she knew that, but she was getting tired of the same lecture over and over ... *and over.*

"By the way, drowning yourself in milk shakes won't make him appear at your doorstep."

And over.

"So what will make him appear?" Tessa asked. "Where exactly does one go to find oneself a buffoon?"

15

Tessa sat in her office and watched as the black car with darkened windows drove into the parking lot of Abbott and Associates.

For the second week in a row, Mr. Abbott had left Tessa alone to work while he was off on client visits. Although he seemed pleased when he periodically checked in, she was only cautiously optimistic his attitude was changing and continued to keep her eyes and ears open for another position. With his Dr. Jekyll/Mr. Hyde personality, she never knew what to expect and hated the feeling of being on edge— wondering when his good mood would suddenly burst into a fit of rage.

Working steadily, she made her way through her to-do list, completing nearly all of the work that had previously piled up. It was exactly what she needed to take her mind off her disappointing weekend. After leaving Holly's on Friday night, she received several texts from Brandon apologizing. At first she thought he might actually have a conscience, although she didn't feel sorry enough for the guy to respond to any of his pleas. On Saturday morning, he asked if they were still on for dinner that evening. *Pig.* She texted back with a simple *go to hell*—then blocked his number. That evening, she took Sophie and went to Ava's, just in case he couldn't take the not so subtle hint and decided to show up anyway for their *date.* Hopefully, Sophie wouldn't need the services of the emergency room again anytime soon—or ever.

She watched as a man got out of the mysterious dark car. He was young, about her age, maybe slightly older, and carried a briefcase that looked like it had seen better days. He was a bit ragged looking; dressed casually, in a simple, somewhat wrinkled, oxford button down shirt and jeans that had frayed at the bottom. His hair was dark, almost black, and was a mess. At first glance, he looked like he had just rolled out of bed or was living out of his car.

She quickly opened up Mr. Abbott's calendar on her computer. Other than the client visits outside of the office, he didn't have any meetings scheduled. Nobody ever came to Abbott and Associates without an appointment ... well, besides the postman, package delivery person, and occasional computer guy, but she recognized all of them. It made Tessa nervous being in the office alone, thanks to a combination of her mother's neurosis that had worn off on her and Ava's attack several years ago. She now wished she'd locked the doors and had a baseball ball bat. At the very least she needed to start carrying some pepper spray.

The front doors opened, and she cautiously rose from her chair. Like a snake approaching her prey, she slowly made her way down the hall toward the reception area, her body hugging the wall while she moved closer to the entrance. Keeping her cell phone in her hands, Tessa had 9-1-1 ready and waiting on the display screen. All she had to do was hit send.

"Hello?" the man called out.

"Can I help you?" Tessa's shaky voice asked as she rounded the corner.

"Yes. Thank you. Is Mr. Abbott here?"

She noticed him looking at the oversized framed portrait of Steven Abbott that hung in the small lobby of their office ... another sign of her boss' inflated ego. Under the photo was a printed canvas with his bio: graduated from the local university with honors over thirty years ago, passed the CPA exam the year he graduated, a list of large firms he'd worked for, awards, blah, blah, blah. Any common criminal could come in here and ask for Mr. Abbott, it didn't prove a thing about this guy's identity or credibility.

He turned his attention back to her from the photo, looking at her strangely, probably wondering why she stood there silently just staring at him with an odd expression. "Are you Tessa?" he asked.

"Yes," she hesitated, noticing his piercing blue eyes under his mop of hair. Okay, he knew her name. What was going on?

"Hi," he said, reaching into his briefcase. "I believe you've been waiting for these?" He held out a thick pile of statements. The name *Nicholas Schilling* was across the top page.

She sighed inwardly. Of course. She'd been so distracted over that idiot doctor, she'd forgotten Mr. Schilling's financial assistant would be delivering the statements this week.

"I'm sorry," she said, trying to calm her racing heart and overactive imagination. "Mr. Abbott's not here." Putting her phone down on the table used for outgoing mail, she took the papers out of the man's hands and tried not to laugh at her foolish behavior. "Thank you, we've been expecting these." It was only a half lie.

She looked at the man who was standing in front of her. Now that she knew he wasn't some common criminal, she couldn't help but notice he also had chiseled cheekbones to go along with his incredible blue eyes. Maybe she did want to apply for that job in Mr. Schilling's office after all.

"If you have questions about any of those reports, just give me a call." He smiled, showing off dimples.

Dimples, too? She couldn't take her eyes off of him. What was going on with her?

"I have some time now, and the conference room is free. If you want to quickly go through them, I mean. That way I won't have to bother you later."

She knew clear as day she didn't need any help going over any statements. In fact, she preferred to work by herself, and working with Schilling's financial assistant without Mr. Abbott's approval would certainly be grounds for dismissal. After the fiasco with Dr. Two-timer, she couldn't explain it. She should be pushing him out the door without giving it a second thought, yet, just the opposite was happening. She suddenly felt ready to hangout with just a normal, unpretentious guy. He was normal, right? So what if he happened to be on the better side of average looking? He didn't seem to notice with that messy thing he had going on. *It was almost buffoonish.* Yes, that was it! Was this the guy who would make her cry?

He smiled back at her. "Sure, I have some time."

16

"So, can I get you anything—water, coffee, a powerbar? I'm afraid we don't keep anything around here to eat, but I could order in sandwiches or something."

Tessa glanced over at Mr. Schilling's financial assistant. They'd been sitting in the conference room, going over statements for the last hour. For someone who looked completely disheveled, this guy was smart. Well, of course he would be. It's not like Mr. Schilling wouldn't hire the best and the brightest. It's just this was an impromptu meeting, and he acted like he'd prepared for weeks. Maybe he was one of those absent-minded professor types. One of those guys who look like they live on the streets, but is in fact an actual genius. One thing was for sure; he didn't smell like he lived on the streets. He smelled good. *Really good.* It was hard not to notice.

"Now that you mention it, I am kind of hungry. I didn't have time to grab breakfast. A sandwich would be great, but only if you let me buy."

"Oh," she said, "thank you. Are you sure?" She hadn't thought about who would be paying for lunch, now that he mentioned it, but she was glad he'd offered. It's not like Mr. Abbott gave her a corporate credit card or anything, and she doubted he'd reimburse her, given the fact he'd be too busy firing her for having this little unplanned meeting. He was very particular when it came to Mr. Schilling's financial information. It didn't matter that this guy was privy to the statements. Her boss wouldn't want anyone going over the numbers until he himself had a chance to rip apart Tessa's projections. Luckily, Mr. Abbott was away at an out of state client's office for the next two days. He'd already called this morning to check in and said he probably wouldn't have a chance to call again until close to five o'clock.

"It's no problem," he replied. "I'll just charge it back to the office. After all, this is a working lunch." He curved the corners of his mouth up, showing off his dimples again. "A very pleasant working lunch," he added.

Feeling the heat rise to her cheeks, she smiled back before shyly looking away. "Let me go find the menu for the nearby deli," she said. "I'll be right back."

She walked down the hall and into the kitchen. Taking a long, deep breath, she grabbed the menu, popped into the ladies room to check her hair and makeup, and promptly returned. Handing it over, she said, "The turkey and roast beef are both pretty good, but I'd stay away from the tuna."

He laughed. "I'll trust your judgment. Just order two of whatever you're getting."

She ordered roast beef sandwiches, chips, and drinks before taking a seat at the conference table to continue going over the statements while they waited for lunch to be delivered. The food came quickly, as did the conversation, which remained professional as they worked.

About halfway through their meal, she realized she didn't actually know this guy's name. Would it be too awkward to ask almost two hours into a meeting? Yes. She'd have to do some investigative work once he left.

After finishing the food and reviewing the last of the statements, Tessa showed him her reports from the previous quarter and gave him a run down on the basics of what would be presented at the next meeting. However, she did not give away any of her trade secrets on how she came up with her projections. Good looking or not, that information was hers alone. Even without that information, he seemed impressed.

"I've seen your reports at past conferences," he said as he threw away the trash from lunch and packed up his briefcase. "They're always very impressive."

"Right." Tessa nodded, feeling a bit embarrassed. "Of course, *you* would be at all of the meetings. How silly of me."

"No, not at all, I'm glad you showed me. I always thought of you more as an assistant to Steven Abbott. I never realized you were the brains behind so much of the work."

She smiled. That figured. Why would her boss give her any of the credit? She was just a lowly employee. Would he even know how to do these projections and reports if she left?

"Well, of course Mr. Abbott reviews and approves everything," Tessa explained.

Why was she defending him? Probably because she didn't want this guy going back to Mr. Schilling to report that his accountant's assistant was the one who did all the work even though he paid Mr. Abbott an exorbitant hourly rate. If that got back to her boss, she'd surely lose her job. She needed to make sure that didn't happen. It was time to play up his role a bit, as much as she hated to do it.

"It's like the theater," she continued. "The director is the brains behind the production, but you still need the actors, musicians, backstage crew, and everyone else to make it all happen. I guess you can say you've now been given a backstage tour. When I used to work

in the theater, people paid extra for that, you know."
She raised her eyebrows, feeling a bit flirtatious.

"Ah, you worked in a theater? I'm actually a huge
fan of theater myself. Maybe we could ..." He stopped
mid-sentence, his eyes looking uncertain.

"Maybe we could?" Tessa repeated, hoping he
would continue.

"Well, I was just thinking. There's a small theater
not far from here that I heard about. The Wynne—"

"—Beckett Theater." Tessa interrupted, smiling
wide. "That's my theater. I mean, that's the theater
where I used to work. I was the assistant director."

"I can see it means a lot to you. Your entire face lit
up just at the mention of it."

Tessa put her hands to her cheeks. "Did it?" she
asked. "I haven't been back there in years."

"Well, they're doing a production of *Guys and
Dolls*. Tomorrow night is the last night. It may sound
kind of funny, but I've always been a fan of shows
from that era. Would you be interested in going?
Perhaps we could have dinner before?"

Tessa beamed. Funny how this guy went from being
someone she was suspicious of to her dream date in
just a matter of hours.

"I'd like that, thank you."

"Great. I'll give you a call tomorrow. I do have to
run, though. I'm so glad I finally had a chance to meet
you." He showed off his dimples one more time as he
grabbed his ratty old briefcase.

"Same," she replied. She watched as he left the building and drove away, before picking up her phone.

"Nicholas Schilling Capital Ventures, how may I direct your call?" the receptionist answered.

"Hello, can you tell me the name of Mr. Schilling's financial assistant, please?"

"Certainly, his name is Todd Mitchell, but I'm afraid he's not in the office at the moment. Would you like his voicemail?"

"No, that's okay, thank you." Sitting back in her chair, she smiled. *Todd Mitchell.* Well now her date had a name.

17

Shortly after Tessa arrived home from work, Holly came over to help her get ready for her date and to stay with Sophie. Apparently her sister still felt guilty about the entire Dr. Scumbag incident, as she wasted no time volunteering to come over.

"Stop fidgeting," she said, gently rubbing her sister's arm as Tessa nervously adjusted the edge of her top for the fifth time. "Everything will be fine, you'll see. Besides, I thought you said you liked this guy."

"I did. I mean, I do. I just … that was yesterday, and now I'm thinking, what if I'm moving too fast?"

Taking her sister's hands in her own, Holly turned Tessa so she was looking directly at her. "Too fast for what? You're having dinner and going to a play. That sounds like a pretty typical first date. That's all it is, sweetie. A date. There's no commitment other than to get out of the house and enjoy someone else's company for a few hours. You're not even letting him pick you up. Which sucks for me, because I was really hoping to meet him."

When Todd had called her during the day to get her address, she made some excuse about having to run an errand first and said she would meet him at the restaurant instead. He already knew where she worked, and she wasn't sure she was ready to give out her home address, nor did she want to be alone in a car with him. What did she really know about him, anyway? She preferred to have her own escape route if need be.

"I know. It's just hard. And I don't think I like what I'm wearing. Stupid small closet and day job."

Getting prepared for her date proved to be no easy feat. After trying on about twenty outfits, she was now wearing a black skirt and blue top that matched her eyes. Everything she owned was either too casual or meant for the office. She really needed to go shopping.

"You look perfect," Holly said with a reassuring tone. "The first outfit looked great. So did the second, third, and fourth. Everything you put on looks great, Tess. Stop second-guessing yourself."

Whatever happened to her carefree days of just throwing something on and walking away? She used to be so confident. She was such a different person now.

"Mommy," Sophie said, tugging at her skirt and looking up at her with adoring eyes, "I think you look like a princess."

Bending down to give her daughter a hug, Tessa smiled. "Aw, thank you, sweetie. I think you look like a princess, too. I promise I won't be out late tonight, and when I get back, I'll come give you a kiss and snuggle, even though you'll already be asleep. You be good for Aunt Holly, okay?"

"She's always good," Holly said, "and we're going to have lots of fun. I brought surprises." Lifting up a tote bag, her sister smiled. "I raided the art room at school today. I've got felt, glitter, Popsicle sticks, fuzzy balls, glue, markers, and all kinds of other fun stuff. Promise we won't make a mess, Mom," she said, sticking her tongue out.

"Wow, maybe I should stay home. It sounds like you're going to have more fun here."

"No way." Holly handed Tessa her purse and keys. "Isn't it time for you to leave? I believe Prince Charming is waiting for you."

Tessa stared at the man sitting across the table from her at the Urban Bistro. *Damn he cleaned up good.* Hair perfectly styled, clothing no longer wrinkled or frayed ... dimples still there. She wiped her palms on her skirt under the table, trying to calm her nerves.

The last time she'd been to the Urban Bistro was several years ago on Valentine's Day with her sister, Holly. They'd both been dateless and needed a place to go that would be free of memories of past boyfriends. It took nearly getting through the entire alphabet before finding a place they could both agree to. They didn't stay. Besides running into the nasty woman Ben was dating at the time, they couldn't even afford to purchase a bottle of water. *Nicholas Schilling really does pay well, doesn't he?*

"Have you been here before?" she asked.

"No, but I've always wanted to check it out. I've heard good things."

She hoped he'd been warned about the prices, and that he was paying for the meal.

"How about you?" he asked. "Do you come here a lot?"

"No," she said, laughing under her breath. "I was here once, years ago with my sister, but haven't been back since." Technically it was true. He didn't need to know they hadn't actually had anything to eat or drink when they came.

The waitress came by with the bottle of wine Todd ordered, filling his glass first, and then hers, after allowing him a chance to give his approval.

"Thank you," he said. "We still need a few moments before ordering."

"Certainly," she acknowledged, walking away quietly.

Todd raised his glass. "To a hopefully not so awkward first date."

Tessa smiled and clinked her glass against his. "Agreed."

"So," he began, after they each took a sip, "assistant director of a community theater to financial guru. That's quite a leap. What brought that on?"

So much for this first date not being awkward, she thought. *Apparently we're getting to the tough topics right from the get-go. Might as well get this over with and watch him race out the door.*

Taking a long sip of her wine, she thought carefully about how to answer. "Well," she began, "theater's my first love. I was a theater production major in college. I was lucky to get a job in my field right out of school."

"Yes, you were. Fresh after graduation, I was slinging burgers, and trust me, it was not my dream job. So why didn't you stick with it?"

She picked up the wine glass again and began swirling the red liquid around the edges slowly. Why was she hesitating? Getting pregnant with Sophie was nothing to be ashamed of. It wasn't her fault Scott couldn't handle the pressure. She loved her daughter more than anything else in this world. If this guy—who was practically a stranger—couldn't handle the fact she had a child, then he wasn't worth her time.

"I'm sorry," he said. "Am I getting too personal too soon? I have a tendency to do that sometimes. I just find you so easy to talk to." He flashed a caring smile at her, and she suddenly felt more at ease.

"No, it's fine." She smiled back. "Sometimes life doesn't turn out quite as we plan, but in the process we wind up with unexpected gifts … amazing gifts, actually. That's what happened to me. My gift is my daughter. Her name is Sophie, and she's three years old. The short story is I needed to find a career that could support the two of us better."

Taking another sip of her wine, she waited for Todd to make up some excuse as to why he had to cut their date short.

"She's lucky to have such a loving and selfless mother. I hope I get to meet her one day."

This time the caring look didn't come from his smile, but came straight from his eyes. It was honest and sincere and traveled directly to her heart.

18

"And so you've always been interested in finance?" Tessa asked as they finished their coffee.

She and Todd had been talking in the restaurant so long, they'd completely lost track of time and missed the play. When they realized what had happened, they decided to order dessert and keep talking. Actually, it was more like Todd asking questions and Tessa doing all of the talking. He seemed fascinated by her history: her background, her sisters, her daughter, her past mistakes. It was as if he needed to absorb every last detail of her life.

She was glad she'd told him about Sophie right away. With the few dates she'd actually had in the past, bringing up the subject of a daughter was always a source of major anxiety. In addition to the timing of when to bring the topic of Sophie up, there was always the how. Plus, she worried incessantly about what her date's reaction might be. What if yet another guy walked out on her?

Not that this was a serious relationship or anything ... it was just one date. *The first date.* Would there be a second?

Tessa finally decided it was her turn to start asking some of the questions. She started with neutral topics about finance in general—interest rates, the stock market, bond yields—safe subjects she knew he'd feel comfortable talking about before asking more personal questions. Just who was Todd Mitchell? He didn't seem to mind being the subject of her interrogation.

"Would you believe my story is similar to yours?" he asked, tilting his head just slightly while raising his eyebrows. His eyes smiled, flirting without words.

Looking at Todd, she giggled. "You have a three year old daughter named Sophie, too?"

"No," he laughed. "I wanted to go into the arts. Music actually. I played guitar and a little piano. In fact, we were probably at the university during the same time, although I didn't take any theater classes."

"And I didn't take any music classes," Tessa told him. "But small world, isn't it? So what was your career plan? Did you have visions of becoming a big time rock star? The next Paul McCartney perhaps?"

Todd shook his head and smirked. "See, now you sound like my mother. That's exactly what she asked me. The answer was, I had no idea. I just knew I loved making music. Period. Past that, I seriously had no clue how a music degree would help me. Eventually, I realized I could play music without a fancy piece of paper signed by the university president. However, I knew I probably wouldn't be able to support myself that way. So I dropped out of the music school and declared finance as my major. I'm not really sure why I picked it to be honest, except my roommate at the time was a finance major, and he seemed to like it. I know, not exactly the preferred method for picking one's path in life, but here I am. It all seemed to have worked out okay."

"I suppose you must have liked it since you've stuck with it."

"I got lucky," he said. "After some initial grunt jobs."

"Like slinging burgers?" Tessa joked.

"Right," he laughed. "Like slinging burgers. Well, after that, I really just was in the right place at the right time. I've been fortunate with how things turned out. What's that saying? Timing is everything? I guess I had fate on my side."

"I used to be a big believer in fate," she said, looking away.

"Not so much anymore, I take it?"

Shaking her head, she felt the sting of tears starting to form. Time to change the subject and quickly. "Do you still play guitar and piano?" she asked, forcing a smile.

"No. Sadly, I haven't picked up my guitar in ages or sat behind a piano."

"Why not?"

"Work. Life. I've been so wrapped up in other things. Talking about rates of returns and stock yields all day hardly gets my creative juices flowing. Maybe I need some new inspiration. Like tonight—tonight has been very inspirational." Even in the dim lighting, she could see a hint of a sparkle shining through his eyes.

"But we *were* sitting here talking about rates of return and stock yields," she reminded him, grateful for the low lighting. She could feel her cheeks getting flushed from his comment.

"Well, somehow coming from you, they seem so much more interesting." He reached across the table placing his hands over hers. A warm surge swept through her body.

She tried to steady her breathing and was grateful that he only held the top of her hands, as her palms were a sweaty mess. When the waitress came by, he let go, giving Tessa the opportunity to take another sip of her coffee before discreetly wiping her hands in her napkin.

"Can I get you two anything else?" she asked.

"No, I think we're all set," Todd replied. "Just the check, please." Turning to Tessa, he said, "I'm sorry we missed the play. It's such a nice night. Would you like to go for a walk in town?"

"That would be great," she replied, putting her hand back on the table. She waited for him to take it again, but the waitress promptly returned. She was grateful when he slid several bills in the leather folder without flinching. "Would you excuse me for a moment?" she asked. "I just need to check in with my sister to make sure Sophie is okay."

"Of course. Take all of the time you need. I'll wait for you by the front door."

"Thank you."

Picking up her phone, she waited until he was far enough away and dialed Holly's number.

"How's it going?" her sister asked as soon as she answered.

"Hello to you, too," Tessa replied laughing. "It's going fine." She knew Holly probably wanted every detail, but didn't want to waste time at the moment since Todd was waiting for her. "I'll fill you in later. How's Sophie?"

"Fast asleep. I wore her out." She stifled a yawn as she talked.

Tessa laughed. "You mean she wore you out." Peeking around the corner, she could see that Todd had his back to her and was gazing out the front window. "Anyway, I'm probably going to be another hour or so. Is that okay? Feel free to crash on my bed or the couch if you want."

"It's no problem. Go have fun."

"Thanks, Hol. I owe you one."

"You owe me more than one, but that's what sisters are for," she replied. "Love you. Be safe."

"Always. Love you, too."

19

Stars lit up the sky as Tessa and Todd made their way toward Forest Hills' quaint downtown area. The streets were crowded for a Tuesday night, with people out window shopping and enjoying the comfortable temperatures, which were unseasonably warm for late February. Perhaps that old groundhog was wrong for once. They could use an early spring after the brutal winter they'd endured.

Despite the brief hand holding in the restaurant, Todd did not reach for her hand as they walked down the street. She didn't know whether to feel disappointed or relieved. Scratch that ... she definitely felt disappointed, although she wished she could be certain her palms were not sweaty. She wiped them against her jacket just in case and hoped the warm breeze would take over to dry them off if necessary.

They managed to keep the conversation going while strolling along. Todd asked if Sophie was okay at home with her sister, and Tessa asked if he had a busy day at work tomorrow. They'd stop at shop windows occasionally to take note of items of interest and, of course, made the obligatory comments about the weather, mentioning what a nice night it was for winter on the East Coast. Both seemed a bit nervous as to where, when, and how the walk would end.

"It's been ages since I've been down this way," Todd told her, looking around. "When I was in college, we used to come down here all of the time. There was a little pub, right here on this corner. The owner used to let me play guitar on Friday nights pretty regularly."

"O'Grady's," Tessa replied, smiling. "I remember it. When I was in school, we used to come out to see a cute boy play guitar here on Friday nights." She stopped in front of the pub that was now a flower shop to study his face. "You were the cute boy?"

"What do you mean *were?*" he teased, smirking just enough to bring out his dimples. "Are you saying I'm not cute anymore?"

"Yes," she replied. "I mean no." She laughed. *Oh, he was definitely still cute.* "I mean ... it's funny I didn't recognize you. We came out to see you all the time. You look so different now."

"Wait a second." He smoothed his hair back, fully exposing his forehead, and parted it on the other side. Then pulled a pair of tortoiseshell eyeglasses from his front pocket and put them on. He positioned his hands as if he were holding a guitar. "How about now?"

"Yes! The glasses are a little different, but there's no doubt about it. You're the cute boy with the guitar!"

"I wear contacts now," he said, pulling off the glasses and fixing his hair. "And yes, the frames are different from the ones I wore back in college. These are actually some reading glasses I picked up in the pharmacy. Even with the contacts I need them for some things. Getting old is so much fun. I probably should have had them on before when we were looking at all those statements, but I left them at home."

"Wow, I can't believe I knew you from then ... well, sort of. I don't think we ever talked or anything. The pub was always so crowded. You really knew how to pack a house."

"I don't think it was me," he said. "It was probably those happy hour prices. Fifty-cent drafts tended to bring college kids in. Even if it was only the crappy stuff in Dixie cups."

"Well, I was there to see you, and now suddenly here we are, back at the pub. Of course, it's a flower shop now, but still. We're back at the same corner.

Stuff like this always blows my mind. My sister, Holly, reconnected with someone she knew in high school years later, and they just got married." She felt her cheeks getting flushed again. "I'm going to shut up now."

Todd grabbed a single pink rose from the canister of colorful flowers on the sidewalk and handed the man a dollar bill.

"For you," he said, holding it out to Tessa.

She smiled. "Pink is my favorite color. Lucky guess?" she asked.

"Maybe," he responded.

She looked down and blushed. "I hope you didn't think when I brought up my sister getting married I was implying we were ... Sometimes I say stuff without thinking first. I was just being silly."

Putting his fingers under her chin, Todd lifted her face back up. "No, not silly at all. Remember what I said at dinner about being in the right place at the right time? That doesn't just have to do with coincidence."

"I told you. I don't believe in that fate stuff anymore," she said.

"What if I can convince you you're wrong? What if I can convince you there's a force that's greater than you and me. Look around you, Tessa. Here we are standing outside the building of the place where we were first brought together. Only we never knew we were supposed to meet for some reason. It took all of these years to figure it out. Maybe fate was trying to tell us we weren't ready yet, you know? You still had to have Sophie, and I still had to get my career started."

Could that be true? Was this fate's doing? She nodded slightly, unable to speak, mesmerized by his words, his eyes, *his lips.*

He continued, still keeping his hand softly resting under her chin. "But now fate brought us back together—to this spot. It means something. The right place at the right time ... I just happened to come to your office yesterday and wind up spending most of the day? Then we eat dinner at a restaurant that's within walking distance from here? I didn't plan that. My intention yesterday was to drop the statements off and leave. I actually had a busy day scheduled and kind of got in trouble for blowing off some important stuff."

"I'm sorry about th—" Tessa started, but Todd put his fingers to her lips to stop her.

"No, it was meant to happen that way. The same way this was ... again completely unplanned. We missed the play and decided to go on this walk, and now, here we are, at the place where maybe we were destined to meet all along years ago, but for some reason didn't. I don't think those are coincidences."

"So what do we do now?" she asked, barely able to get the words out.

"I think I'm supposed to kiss you," he replied, leaning in to her waiting lips

20

"That's just the most romantic thing I think I've ever heard," Holly said, once Tessa finally got home that evening and retold the events leading up to the kiss outside of what used to be O'Grady's Pub. "You know me, I'm a big believer in fate and destiny. Why do you think I got so hung up on Ben when he suddenly reappeared everywhere in town after Ava's wedding?"

"Um, because Jared turned out to be a complete loser? And, if I remember correctly, *I'm* the one who had to convince *you* it was fate that Ben kept showing up. You were the one who kept saying *if anything the universe is trying to tell me I'm meant to be with*

Jared, blah, blah, blah. Yeah, how'd that work out for you?" She smirked and shook her head. "Funny how your memory seems to have changed over the years."

"Oh, yeah, right. I can't believe I actually wanted to marry that guy." Holly shuddered. "Luckily, something kept nagging at me, telling me there was a reason Ben was back in my life. I just couldn't shake it. Fate has a way of letting you know when the timing is just right."

"That's kind of what Todd said."

"He sounds like a smart guy. A smart guy who believes in fate. So what happened after your magical kiss? Did the walls come back at record speed like they usually do to lock you in and throw away the key? Poor guy."

Tessa rolled her eyes. "It was a nice date. I'm not saying I gave him a key, but the door is definitely unlocked at the moment."

"Oh really?" Holly asked, raising her eyebrows. "And yet, here you are, still standing in one piece without the world crumbling around you. Dare I say you're even smiling ... glowing perhaps? Come on, you know I love it when you admit I'm right."

"You were wrong about the doctor," she said, grinning.

"Okay, well, I can't win them all. However, you do have to admit that he got you back on the market, so in that respect, I was right."

"How so?" Was Holly really going to stand there and rationalize that showing interest in a married man was a good thing?

"Because, before Dr. Sleazeball, you were just sitting home every night, not even willing to consider dating anyone anymore. I mean, you had a few dates here and there after Scott, but it's been at least a year now since your last date if I remember correctly, and it wasn't with anyone you even seemed remotely interested in. Anyway, the doctor, while not the most ideal candidate for you—"

"You can say that again," Tessa mumbled.

Holly sighed. "I'm just saying he got your emotions stirring and open to dating again, that's all. Otherwise, you probably wouldn't have given this Todd guy the time of day, and we wouldn't be having this conversation."

Smiling, she nodded. "I suppose you're right."

"What was that? I didn't get that," her sister said, putting her hand to her ear.

Tessa sighed a loud, dramatic sigh. "I said perhaps you *maybe* could have been correct in this one situation."

"Oh, wait a second." Holly grabbed a piece of paper and pen out of her purse. "There are no witnesses here. Would you mind jotting that down for me, and then just sign and date at the bottom. Or anywhere on the paper." She smiled wide as she handed both items over to her sister.

"I used to do this to you back when I was trying to get you and Ben together, didn't I? I can now see I might have been a tad bit annoying."

"Yes." She grinned. "Paybacks are a bitch. Go ahead, I'm still waiting on that signature."

"Don't you have to get up early for work, Holly?" Tessa asked, gently pulling her out of her chair and pushing her toward the door.

"No," she replied, picking up her purse and her coat on the way. "It's really not that late. You still haven't told me what happened after the kiss. When you called from the restaurant, you said you'd be home in an hour, and now it's three hours later. A lot can happen in three hours. Care to share?"

"*What? What's that, Ben? Yes, your wife's on her way home right now.*" Tessa opened her front door and eased her sister out into the hallway.

"Come on, sis. I live four miles away. You can't hear Ben calling for me. I'd tell you! You know I would."

"Thanks again for watching Sophie, Hol. I really do appreciate it. Be careful getting home. Love you." She softly closed the door, leaving her sister standing in the hallway of her apartment building.

"Love you, too!" Holly called from the other side. "And glad you had a great date!"

Standing with her back against the door, Tessa couldn't help but smile. After the kiss that had left her both speechless and breathless, Todd did in fact take her hand in his again. They walked until the end of the strip of shops, stopping occasionally to sneak into a back alley for more kisses. When the shops ran out, they followed the path along the river, finding a bench to sit on where they talked, held hands, and kissed some more. The path eventually looped back around to where their cars were parked at The Urban Bistro.

"I can't ever remember feeling like this after a first date," Todd had said, cupping Tessa's face in his hands before lowering his lips down to meet hers once more.

She melted under his touch, trying to savor the feel of his lips, knowing the evening was coming to an end. *Was he going to ask her out again?* She hoped a second date would be in their future. She wouldn't have to wait long to find out.

"Can I see you again?" he asked, pushing her hair out of her eyes.

"Yes," she said softly, trying to maintain her balance. Just the slightest touch of his hands on her face made her knees weak.

"I'm free this weekend. Would Friday night be okay? Maybe we can actually make it to a play this time." He smiled, leaning in to nip playfully at her curled back lips.

"That sounds perfect," she replied as he straightened back up.

Holding her door open, he gave her another tender kiss just before she slid into the driver's seat.

"Until Friday then," he said, blowing her a kiss as she started her engine and drove away.

21

"**O**-kay, these weren't here five minutes ago," Tessa said to herself quietly as she walked into her office upon coming back from the restroom. She bent down to smell the enormous bouquet of assorted pink flowers sitting in a beautiful crystal vase in the middle of her desk, which a delivery person must have left when she stepped out momentarily. Taking in the amazing aroma, she spotted the small card sticking out among the sea of pink petals and picked it up to read.

Can't stop thinking about you.

"He didn't sign it," she said, bending down once more to take another whiff, although it really wasn't necessary, as the fragrance had now filled the room. "They must be from—"

"Must be from me?" the voice said, finishing her sentence.

"Oh shit, you startled me!" Tessa exclaimed as Todd entered her office. Jumping back, she nearly knocked over the entire bouquet. She put her hand on her chest as if that would control her erratic heartbeat. "What are you doing here?"

"Well, the business excuse is I found some more statements to drop off. But, the truth is, I couldn't wait until Friday to see you again. And since it appears Mr. Abbott is once again out of the office …" He stepped forward and slid his arm around her waist, pulling her in for a kiss as she wrapped her arms around his neck.

"The flowers are beautiful," she said, drawing away slowly, her breathing now perfectly calmed. "Thank you. I have the one you gave me last night in some water on my kitchen table. When Sophie woke up this morning, she was so excited to see it. She said the color reminded her of the dress Princess Aurora wears."

"I'm sorry," Todd said, looking confused. "I'm afraid I don't get a chance to be around little girls very often. Princess who?"

Tessa laughed. "You've heard of Sleeping Beauty?"

"Ah, yes. Isn't she the one who had some sort of evil curse put on her that could only be broken by the handsome prince?"

"Well," she laughed even harder, "you just described pretty much every Disney movie involving princesses. But yes, technically that is correct. Her curse was that she would forever sleep unless kissed by her prince charming. Her *real* name is Princess Aurora. Sophie's obsessed with her. You scored big points with my daughter by giving me a flower that matched the color of her dress."

"Oh, well, I planned that, of course." He winked. "And what about Sophie's mom?" he asked, still holding his hands lightly on Tessa's waist. "Did I score any points with her?"

"Yes, many," she said, leaning in for another kiss. The piercing ring of the telephone abruptly broke them apart, and she reluctantly reached for the receiver. "Abbott and Associates," she answered, trying not to sound too breathy.

"Do you have the numbers I asked for?" the brusque voice demanded.

"Y-yes, sir," Tessa replied, trying to regroup. She slipped back behind her desk and began typing at her keyboard. Sitting in one of the chairs facing her, Todd smiled and watched as she worked. She was completely flustered now. Where was that file she had out just moments ago?

"I'm waiting, Tessa!" Mr. Abbott bellowed.

Apparently his good mood was starting to wear off.

"I have them right here, sir. I can read them to you over the phone, or would you like me to email or fax them to you instead?"

"What do you think?" he replied snidely.

Was this a trick question? She had no idea. If she told them to him over the phone and he wrote them down wrong, she'd get blamed for that. So no. The fax machine where he was located might not be confidential, so no on that one also. He was calling her from his smart phone, so email it was. "I'll email them right over," she said, proud of her rational thought process.

"I don't have time for that. The client's waiting!" he hollered. "Just give me the damn figures."

She sighed. "Yes, sir." She read him the numbers *and* followed them up with an email so he'd have them in writing as well, more to cover her back than anything else.

Hanging up the phone, she put her head down on her desk. *How humiliating.*

"He's in a good mood," Todd noted. "Sorry. He was yelling so loud, it was hard not hear."

She lifted her head and rolled her eyes. "It would probably be inappropriate for me to comment, you know, given the business relationship you have with him. I'm sure in your meetings he's very pleasant."

"He is. I didn't realize there was another side to him. Business can be very cut throat at times. Some people think they have the right to act a certain way behind closed doors, especially toward woman. I'm personally not a fan. I don't think it gets you anywhere. It certainly won't help you get ahead."

"If it's all the same to you, I'd rather his little outburst just stay between us," Tessa requested. "I don't want to upset the status quo at your office. If Mr. Abbott found out I was bad mouthing him, I could lose my job. Between you and me, I'm looking around for something else, but until I find that something else, I need to stay here. This job may be a little rough at times, but it pays the bills. Well, it pays most of the bills. And I do actually enjoy the work."

"Don't worry," Todd said. "Mum's the word. Besides, you weren't bad mouthing him at all. Half of Forest Hills could probably hear him screaming. In any event, the last thing I want is for you to get fired. I selfishly like being able to hand deliver statements here just so I can see you. In fact, give me that one back." He picked up the statement he'd brought and shoved it back into his briefcase.

"What? Why are you taking that? I need it!"

"I know you do, but I need an excuse to come again tomorrow. So you'll have to wait one more day."

"Oh really?" Tessa asked. "And what about the day after that?"

"That's Friday … our date night."

"You've got it all figured out I see."

An alarm on his phone beeped just as he seemed to be about to say something more. "I've got a meeting I've got to rush off to." He took her hands in his own and kissed her, pressing his body tightly into hers. His phone beeped a second time, and he slowly backed up, leaving her feeling flushed and light-headed. "I'll see you tomorrow," he said, kissing her nose lightly.

"Yes, tomorrow," she repeated, as she sank down into her chair, barely able to move.

22

The theater lights went on as the actors took their final curtain call. Tessa wiped the tears from her eyes.

"It was a comedy," Todd noted. "Why are you crying?"

She smiled. "I just miss it, being here in the theater. It's where I belong. Come on, let's go backstage. I recognize half of the names of the stage crew listed in the program."

Grabbing Todd's hand, she led him down the aisle, against the flow of people leaving the theater. Once next to the stage, she pushed open the heavy black door marked no-admittance and navigated the dark passageways that led back behind the curtains.

"Ah-ha! I knew it!" she shrieked, jumping into the arms of a balding, thin man wearing thick black-framed eyeglasses. "Jim Fergo, that production had your direction written all over it."

"Tessa? Tessa Haines?" he asked, pushing her back slightly to look at her. "Well, look at you! I haven't seen you in forever. You know you were my favorite assistant director." He looked around and whispered, "The assistant director I have now is a complete mess. Please tell me you're here to ask for your job back."

Shaking her head, she shrugged. "Sorry, Jim. We just came to see the show and say hello. This is my ... um ... my—"

"Her boyfriend," Todd interjected.

Tessa glanced at him and smiled. That sounded nice. It was only their second date, but they'd seen and talked with each other every day since they'd met earlier in the week on Monday. *Wow, had it only been four days?*

"Yes, my boyfriend, Todd Mitchell. Todd, this is my former boss, Jim Fergo."

"Nice to meet you," he said, holding out his hand for a shake.

Jim ignored the outstretched arm and pulled Todd into a hug instead, patting him on the back before letting him go. "Nice to meet you, too," he said, slapping him on the back one more time.

Todd looked a bit surprised, but seemed to recover quickly. "Can you imagine if Mr. Abbott greeted everyone that way?" he asked Tessa, laughing.

"That's my new boss," she explained to Jim. "He doesn't do hugs or smiles or much of anything that doesn't involve a scowl."

"Sounds like a real stand-up kind of guy. Are you sure you don't want your old job back?" Jim asked again.

"I'd love my old job back," Tessa replied, "if you can match my current salary and offer benefits."

He shook his head. "We just took a huge hit and had to cut everyone's wages. The assistant director is making less now than when you had the job. And benefits? The only benefits we get around here are free pizza and beer after shows. By the way, help yourselves." He motioned with his head to the table against the wall lined with food and drinks.

"Tessa?"

She turned toward the familiar voices. "Lexie! Alyce! How are you two?"

The three girls embraced as Todd stood to the side with Jim. Grabbing each of the women's hands in her own, she turned to face the men.

"Todd, these are two of the finest sound engineers you'll ever meet."

"Oh, stop," Lexie said. "We only did such a great job because we were working under your direction."

Jim cleared his throat loudly, and the girls looked up at him.

"Now, Jim, you know we love you, too," Lexie started, "but you're focused on the actors and actresses. Tessa was the one directing us most of the time, and you know it. Let her have some of the credit, will you?"

"Are you kidding? Is there a moment in any production where her name doesn't come up? I'm constantly giving her credit," Jim told them.

Tessa looked at her three former co-workers. "Seriously?"

"It's true," Alyce said. "It's no wonder we haven't been able to keep an assistant director around. You're a tough act to follow."

"Hey, do you want to come out with us?" Lexie asked. "We still hang out at Hart's after every show."

"That sounds like fun," Todd said. "What do you say, Tessa? Do you want to join them?"

"Actually, can we do it another time? I'm kind of beat tonight. It was great seeing you, though." She hugged Lexie, Alyce, and Jim, said her good-byes, promising to stay in touch, and took Todd's hand, leading him out the back exit door.

He pulled her to a stop when they reached the next block.

"Are you okay? You seemed so happy in there, and then suddenly, not so happy. What's going on?"

She hung her head down so he couldn't see how truly sad she really was. "I guess it's pretty much like you said. At first I was ecstatic seeing everyone."

He grabbed her around the waist and pulled her in tight. "Anyone could see how much all of that meant to you. Your eyes lit up as soon as you stepped foot in there. They got even brighter when we walked backstage. It was as if you were a completely different person. You were positively glowing. And then, suddenly it all drained away. Why?"

"Because I remembered. That was my life, my passion, but it's not my life anymore ... and it can never be again. I had to give that all up to support Sophie and myself. I guess it's just a dream and not meant to be."

"You don't know that, Tessa. Why can't you have it all? It's important to believe in your dreams. You have to stay positive and trust yourself. If I didn't think that way, I'd probably still be slinging those burgers. Dreams come true, I know they do. I'm living proof."

Tessa looked up into Todd's caring eyes. He meant well, she knew he did, but he wasn't living proof.

"How can you say that?" she asked. "You wanted to be a musician, and you're stuck in the financial industry, too. How are your dreams coming true?"

"I realized that sometimes, old dreams lead us to new dreams. I actually love what I do now. I can't imagine doing anything else, and that includes being a musician. In fact, I'm more convinced than ever, I would have hated that life. That wasn't truly my dream. Do you want to know my dream?" He released Tessa's waist and took her hands in his. Gazing directly at her, he said the words he really didn't even have to say. His eyes said it all. "This. You're part of my dream. Finding someone like you. I know we're only getting to know each other, but I can't remember ever feeling this way. I can't remember, ever being happier."

23

"You've been dating this guy for three weeks now," Ava said as the sisters once again gathered in her kitchen. Sophie was off playing with Logan, while Jenna was upstairs listening to music. Pulling the freshly made chocolate cake out of her oven, she set it on the counter to cool. "I think that's a record for you."

"Well, at least since Scott left me if that's what you mean," Tessa said, taking a seat next to Holly at the table. "It's okay. You can say his name. I was over him the day he walked out on us."

"I know, sweetie," Ava said, sitting down and taking her sister's hand. "I also know the past few years haven't been easy on you. From everything you've told me, Todd sounds like a great guy."

Tessa looked at both of her sisters and forced a smile.

"You see that?" Holly asked, directing her question to Ava. "That's what I'm talking about. That's not an *I'm head over heels happy* smile. That's an *I'm only marginally happy because I can't fully open my heart* smile. What gives, Tessa? You've got the perfect guy. You even said so yourself the other day when we met for dinner after work."

"I know," she said. "Todd is a great guy, really, he is."

"Then what's the problem? You should be walking around with a goofy smile on your face instead of looking like the Queen of Doom, wondering if the world's about to come crashing down."

Tessa rolled her eyes. "I just ... What if he's not perfect? I thought Scott was, and he walked out on us."

Holly sighed. "Honey, no one truly is. I can spend the rest of the night listing off all of Ben's *stuff,* and I'm sure Ava can do the same for Max, but we still love them, because they are perfect for *us.* Anyway, *perfect* was really just a metaphor. What I meant was that he seems like a normal guy. A normal, nice guy who really likes you. There's nothing wrong with that."

"Exactly!" Tessa stated. "He's nice. Too nice. And like you said, everyone has *something.* "

"So now you don't like him because there's nothing wrong with him?" Holly asked. "I can't figure you out sometimes. Anyway, you're in that new googly-eyed stage. He could do just about anything, minus being married like that scuzzy doctor, of course, and you'd still think he was pretty awesome. He's a guy. Eventually you'll notice socks left on the floor or toenails in the tub or *something*. For now, enjoy it."

She shook her head. "No. Twice now he's acted like he's had something to tell me—something important— but he keeps getting interrupted or distracted, and he doesn't come back to it. I keep thinking maybe his *stuff* is more than dirty socks on the floor or toenails in the tub. What if I do let myself fall head over heels, and he just breaks my heart?"

"What if he doesn't, but you walk away before giving him a chance to prove it to you?" Holly asked. "Sounds to me like maybe he's trying to tell you how much he cares about you. You know, the *L word?* Guys always get weird and nervous when they try to say it for the first time."

"Yup, that's what it sounds like to me," Ava agreed. "And if you shut him out now, you'll have missed out on finding the one person who was maybe meant to grab on to your heart ... to share it for the rest of your life. Isn't it worth the risk?"

Tessa took a deep breath, letting it out slowly. "Is it?" she asked. "What's so wrong with being single anyway? Why do I *have* to have someone else in my life?"

Ava stood up to get three plates. *Just like Mom,* Tessa thought. Whenever Tessa asked a tough question, Mom would offer food instead of an answer. She supposed that's where Ava learned most of her cooking skills. Mom always was a fabulous chef. Apparently her three girls asked a lot of difficult questions over the years. Now that Mom wasn't around as much, it seemed Ava was taking over the official role of *comfort food provider.* She placed a large piece of chocolate cake in front of Tessa.

"Here's what I know," Holly started, apparently ignoring that last question. "Every time I've spoken to you over the last three weeks, all you've talked about is Todd."

"Same here," Ava said, smiling and giving Holly a piece of cake as well before sitting back down.

"Whether you want to admit it or not, you've already started falling," her sister continued. "The question is, how far are you willing to fall? If you stop now, will you simply be able to get up and walk away? Honestly?"

Tessa put her head back and closed her eyes. *Honestly? No.* At this point, she couldn't imagine her life without Todd. He was the first person to call her every morning and the last person to call her every night. While their intimacy was still limited to kissing, she'd never felt closer to any man before ... ever. She'd made it clear she wanted to take things slow, and Todd never once pressured her for anything more, despite their obvious desires.

"He wants to meet Sophie."

"That's a big step," Ava told her. "And a good sign."

"What if it doesn't go well?" Tessa asked. "There's no way I could have a relationship with someone who doesn't connect with Sophie and vice versa."

"Then I guess you'll have your answer," Holly responded. "Keep in mind, though, kids are funny and very protective. You and Sophie have a strong bond."

"Holly's right," Ava agreed. "It may take Sophie a few tries to really warm up to him. Don't use Sophie as an excuse to cut Todd out of your life just because they don't hit it off right away. Give them a fair chance. Give *him* a fair chance. He deserves that much. You both do."

"And hey, if they get along, maybe you'll actually let us meet him one day soon, too," Holly added. "We promise we won't scare him away."

24

A t ten in the morning the following Saturday, Tessa and Sophie met Todd at the playground in their neighborhood. She figured it was better to meet at a place where her daughter felt comfortable. That way if she didn't like Todd, she could go off and play without being completely traumatized. Sophie that is ... Tessa had already convinced herself the entire experience would be traumatic whether her daughter liked Todd or not.

She hadn't told Sophie why they were going to the park until they started on their walk. She was nervous her daughter would be anxious, or maybe she was the one who was anxious. Yes, it was definitely her. Sophie seemed indifferent, or perhaps she didn't understand. After all, Tessa didn't exactly come out and say, "*Sweetie, today you're going to meet the man who potentially could be your future daddy.*" She giggled softly to herself at the thought of how ridiculous that would have sounded. No, instead she said, "*Sophie, we're going to the park to meet a new friend of Mommy's. His name is Todd, and he's very nice. I think you're going to like him a lot.*"

When Tessa finished explaining, Sophie shrugged and said, "Okay."

For some reason, she expected her daughter to have a million questions. Instead, she rambled on about a book they had read in preschool the day before. It was about a mouse named Jason who sang all these silly songs. Smiling, Tessa watched as her daughter skipped and hummed for the remainder of the walk.

Todd was already waiting for them when they arrived. She was a nervous wreck. Before they left, she'd changed her outfit at least a dozen times. He, on the other hand, seemed completely at ease. She supposed that was a good sign.

Sophie hid behind her leg as she introduced them. Besides her uncles, Max and Ben, and her grandfather, she didn't have a lot of men in her life. Tessa knew she'd be shy and cautious, and perhaps as Holly suggested, even protective.

"It's very nice to meet you, Sophie," Todd said, squatting down so he could look her in the eyes. "Your mom told me so much about you. She even told me pink is your favorite color."

She nodded, still keeping one arm securely wrapped around her mother's leg. Sneaking out for a peek at the pink gift bag Todd was holding, she quickly took to hiding again.

"Oh, you didn't have to get her anything," Tessa said, feeling a little embarrassed. *Was he trying to buy her affections? Or was this just part of his niceness?*

He smiled. "I know that, but a funny thing happened yesterday. I was at a meeting downtown, and as I was walking back to my car, I passed a store where something in the window caught my eye. I don't have any little girls myself, so I thought it was odd I noticed it at all. However, it was so beautiful, and I thought, *I'll bet Sophie would like this.*" He handed the bag to her.

"For me?" she asked, still clutching her mom's leg.

He nodded. "Yes."

"Go ahead, it's okay," Tessa told her.

He put the bag on the ground in between them as a peace offering and waited as Sophie slowly approached. Reaching for the bag with widened eyes, she carefully took out the pink tissue paper lying on top.

"Mommy! Look!" She pulled out a beautiful doll dressed in a pink dress; the exact color of the flower Todd gave Tessa on their first date. "It's Princess Aurora!"

"Is it?" he asked. Tessa caught his eye just as he winked at her. "She's very beautiful, just like you. I hope you like her."

"I do, I do!" She twirled the doll around in her hands, unable to take her eyes off of her perfectly styled golden hair and bright, silky clothes. Seemed poor Daisy would be getting shelved for a while.

"Sophie," Tessa said, "what do you say?"

"Thank you!" she shrieked. "I love her." She gave the doll a huge hug and smiled coyly at Todd, no longer feeling the need to hide behind her mom's leg.

"You're very welcome." he said, standing back up. "It's such a nice day, what do you think about going to the zoo after we play here for a little bit?"

"Can we, Mommy?" she begged, still clutching her doll. "Please?"

Tessa beamed. She couldn't believe he'd made such a perfect suggestion. Princess Aurora was somewhat easy, *incredibly thoughtful*, but easy. She had told him early on that Sophie loved her. Although she was more than impressed he actually remembered since she'd only mentioned it once three weeks ago. She figured he would have filed that under *can't be bothered to remember*. But the zoo? She never mentioned that her daughter's favorite place to visit was the Forest Hills Zoo. Not once. She also never mentioned they hadn't been there in ages ... not since they raised their rates. It was too expensive for Tessa.

Of course, didn't most kids love the zoo? Maybe he wanted to find something to do that wouldn't involve much interaction with her; something where she could run around, look at the animals, and seem happy. Sophie in a good mood certainly would make *him* look good, too. *No. Stop trying to find something wrong with him, and enjoy the fact that you really did find an amazing guy.*

"Yes, sweetie. I think the zoo sounds like a wonderful idea," she replied, feeling as though the day might just work out all right after all.

25

"So," Ben said as he finished setting the table, "I
hear you've got a man in your life now. A
single guy this time." He winked.

It was Sunday night, the day after the zoo outing
with Todd. Tessa had wanted to call her sisters as
soon as she got home from her amazing day, but
something had kept her from being overly excited
about it. *Damn walls.* Instead, she waited for Ava and
Holly to call her the next morning. When she was light
on details, Holly invited her over for dinner,
presumably to try to get more out of her. She
wondered if Ava was in on the plan, too. Probably.

She wouldn't be surprised if this entire get together was Ava's idea.

"Very funny, *Dad,*" Tessa teased as she took a seat. "Don't worry, he's from a very respectable family. As far as I know, his father gets out of prison next year, and his mother only has to work the streets every other weekend."

"Ah, he sounds like a fine chap," he continued, joining her, "a stellar member of society. Excellent work. We're all so proud."

"Actually," Holly explained, placing down the salad bowl, "from what Tessa has told me so far, he's a true gentleman."

"I'm sorry to hear that. So no action in the bedroom yet, huh, Tess?"

"Benjamin!" Holly glared at her husband and threatened him with the dishtowel she loved to swipe him with. "That's none of your business. Oh, you men are all the same."

"So ... how about this weather, eh?" Tessa asked, taking a gulp of water and trying to control her blushing cheeks.

"Just ignore him," Holly said, peeking around the corner to where Sophie sat playing on the floor with her new doll. "She looks happy. I take it everything went well yesterday?"

Tessa smiled. *Here we go.* "Yes, it was very nice."

"That's it? Very nice?" Holly asked. "That's all you're going to give me?"

"Ben, can I ask you a question?" she asked, taking another long sip of her drink.

"Shoot," he replied.

"If you were meeting the three year old child of the woman you were dating for the first time, what would you have planned for the day?"

"Well," he said, rubbing his forehead, "let's see. I guess if it's nice out, we could try to find a park with a playground or something. Maybe bring a Frisbee or a soccer ball so I could play with her child for a while … you know, so we could try to bond and get comfortable with each other. Afterwards, we could go to a family friendly restaurant for some lunch. One of those places where they give the kids a couple of crayons and a placemat with activities on it—that way, the little one is happy, and I can enjoy a nice meal with the mom." Ben sat back in his chair seemingly proud of himself.

Tessa looked at him and smiled.

"You're not saying anything," he remarked with a concerned expression. "Is that an okay answer? Did I pass?"

Walking over to her husband, Holly gave him a kiss on his cheek. "I think that sounds wonderful, honey. Just don't let me ever catch you dating any women with three year olds, and we won't have any problems."

"Does that mean I can date women who don't have three year olds?" he asked with a big smile on his face.

He ducked just as the dishtowel came flying through the air.

"And what about Princess Aurora? Do you know anything about her?" Tessa asked Ben, ignoring the playful banter between her sister and her husband.

"I never touched her! I swear!" He looked at Holly and shielded his head.

"How about a gift?" Tessa continued, trying to stay serious to get a straight answer out of the one male beside her father she really trusted. "Would you think of bringing the three year old you were meeting for the first time a gift?"

"No. To be honest, that thought didn't cross my mind, but it's a nice touch."

Holly finished placing the last of the dinner preparations on the table and grabbed her own drink before sitting down. "So what's with all of the questions? Are you going to tell us what happened yesterday?"

Tessa smiled. She filled her sister and brother-in-law in on the significance of Princess Aurora and Todd's choosing of the zoo. "At first I thought maybe he picked the zoo because it would keep Sophie occupied, and he wouldn't have to interact much with her, but it wasn't like that at all. To be honest, I kind of felt like the odd man out."

"How so?" Holly asked.

"Well, for starters, he didn't hold my hand or kiss me once the entire time the three of us were together. I guess he didn't want Sophie to feel uncomfortable. His attention was one hundred percent on her all day. He stopped with her at every exhibit, teaching her about each animal, reading the plaques to her, explaining their habitats, and answering her questions. He was like her own personal tour guide, and she totally ate it up."

"Wow, he put my hypothetical date to shame," Ben said, shaking his head.

"Well, he did do the playground thing also before we left for the zoo. At the one in my neighborhood Sophie loves so much. He pushed her on the swings and went on the slide with her. He even went on that spinning thing." Tessa cringed. "He looked a bit green after, but he was still laughing. So was Sophie. They were so engaged with each other. It makes me wonder if maybe I don't give her enough attention."

"No, of course you do, sweetie," Holly reassured. "Kids are just funny that way when they're around someone new. And the fact that she even allowed him to play with her is huge. I think it's great they seemed to enjoy each other's company so much. In fact, it's the best possible outcome for the day."

"I know," Tessa said, smiling. "She's already asking when we're going to get together with him again. Now I'm doubly afraid."

"Why?" her sister asked, looking confused.

"Aunt Holly!" Sophie came skipping into the kitchen holding out her doll. "Did you see my new

Princess Aurora doll? Mommy's new friend, Todd, gave her to me. We went to the zoo yesterday and saw the baby monkeys. They were so cute. I hope we get to go back again soon. I had the best day ever!"

Tessa watched as Sophie skipped back into the other room before continuing. "Because now he has the power to break two hearts instead of one."

26

"More flowers?" Mr. Abbott stepped inside of Tessa's office with a scowl on his face.

He'd been going out on client visits less and less over the last two weeks, which unfortunately for Tessa meant Todd had been stopping by less and less. They'd decided it was best for him not to drop by when her boss was in the office, knowing it would just cause trouble for her.

"This guy is getting to be a bit much don't you think?" her boss continued.

Was she supposed to answer that? And how? The question seemed ridiculous. Did he think he could control every aspect of her life?

Todd had been sending flowers every few days since their first date six weeks ago. It was as if he had a standing order with the flower shop to know exactly when the last batch would begin to wilt. Each order was different, but was always pink and had card that was just one line—usually something about enjoying the time he spent with her. They were never signed, which was a good thing, because on more than one occasion, she'd caught her boss sneaking a peek at them, no doubt trying to figure out who this mystery man was. Mr. Abbott had no idea the flowers were from his biggest client's financial assistant. Neither of them was sure how he'd react to her mixing business with pleasure, especially where his most lucrative client was concerned. The same went for Mr. Schilling, who didn't know about their relationship either. While Todd thought he would probably be more tolerant of their connection, Tessa didn't want to risk the chance that he might say something about it to Mr. Abbott. Todd agreed not to mention anything to him. So far it seemed their secret remained under wraps.

Speaking of Todd's boss, the all-important quarterly meeting was now a pre-quarter meeting, and it was quickly approaching. Apparently this Schilling guy was feeling antsy and didn't want to wait until the quarter end for someone to reassure him that his millions of dollars were still collecting boatloads of interest and dividends.

Tessa still had so much work to do. As was the case before she'd met Todd, many of the statements were sent over electronically. He was unable to hand deliver them now with her boss back in the office regularly. Well, he *could* have hand delivered them; it wouldn't have been *completely* out of the ordinary. After all, he was Mr. Schilling's assistant and delivering statements wasn't out of the realm of his job duties. Tessa and Todd were just worried they wouldn't be able to hide their feelings for each other in front of Mr. Abbott, should he suddenly appear. Even with her theater degree, there was only so much acting she could manage.

She decided to ignore her boss' last remark and change the subject. "I believe I have everything I need to finalize Mr. Schilling's projections. I should have the preliminary reports for your review by the end of the day tomorrow."

"I would hope so," he commented. "Lord knows you've had plenty of time to work on this. Or have you been too busy with flower arrangements?"

So it was going to be one of *those* days.

"No," Tessa replied smugly, "the flower shop takes care of that for me."

Mr. Abbott narrowed his already beady eyes and stated, "Three o'clock tomorrow and not a minute later. Our meeting is on Thursday, and if these reports are anything like your last batch, you'll need time to redo them all." He turned on his heels, but quickly turned back around to face her again. "On second thought, you might as well clear your evening schedule for the next few nights. I have a feeling you'll be working late. And arrange for a babysitter now. I don't want you bringing that kid of yours around this time." He spun on his heels once more and stormed away.

Oh how she wished she could storm out as well ... *forever.* Of course, she wasn't going anywhere at the moment. Besides the fact she had nowhere to go and had too many bills to pay, she knew that leaving days before a big conference would put a huge strain on Todd's job, since he relied on her reports from the meetings as Schilling's right hand man. However, once this was over, she wasn't going to let Mr. Abbott's *post-meeting* shift in personality slow down her job hunt. She needed out. Her job search plotting ended at the sound of her phone ringing.

"Good morning, Abbott and Associates," she answered, putting on as cheerful of a voice as she could manage after that infuriating exchange.

"Good morning, beautiful. Can you talk?"

Her anger and hostility instantly left her body at the sound of his voice. "I'm so sorry," she replied, trying to sound professional, "I'm still working on that, but let me see what I can do." She began typing on her keyboard, well aware that Mr. Abbott was listening to her every word. In actuality, she was looking at her boss' calendar for the day. "Ah, yes, here we go. It looks like the calculated yield on that bond is 3.5%.

Did you want me to check on any dividends for you?" Tessa smiled, proud of the code she and Todd put together. Bond yields corresponded to appointments when Mr. Abbott would be out of the office, while stock dividends meant he'd be in meetings or conference calls in the office. A 3.5% yield told Todd he'd be away at 3:30.

Todd sighed. "Oh, I'd like nothing more than to calculate some yields with you at 3.5%, but I'm afraid I'm going to be in a meeting myself. How about dinner instead? I can bring something over to your place tonight?"

"Yes," she replied, trying to control her fluttering heart. "I think that sounds fine. It was very nice speaking with you. If you have any additional questions, please don't hesitate to call. Have a great day."

"You too, sweetheart. I can't wait to see you."

She hung up the phone and smiled. Might as well enjoy dinner tonight since it seemed inevitable there would be long nights of work ahead later in the week. Picking the phone back up, she called Ava to make arrangements for babysitting—just in case.

27

Tessa couldn't help but chuckle as she opened her apartment door. Todd clumsily balanced four grocery bags in his arms, with another two on the ground by his feet.

"You know there's only three of us here, right?" She helped take the packages out of his arms before their dinner wound up all over her apartment floor.

"I may have gone a little overboard," he said, "but a new gourmet market opened downtown, and they have all of these pre-packaged fresh meals. I'm afraid I'm not much of a cook, and everything looked so good. I couldn't decide, so I bought one of everything."

Placing the bags on her small kitchen table, she couldn't believe the amount of food being brought in for one night. Her eyes widened as she lifted out each container. He must have spent a small fortune. She'd have to work a month or two to afford all of this gourmet food and forgo paying any other bills such as rent or utilities. She and Sophie would be homeless, but well fed.

"Chicken Parmesan, Shrimp Scampi, Beef Enchiladas, Striped Bass, Lamb Chops, Lobster Tails ... Fillet Mignon? Did I mention I decided to become a vegetarian today?" she teased.

Todd smirked. "No problem. In this bag," he started, pulling out more containers, "we've got grilled zucchini, honey glazed carrots, sautéed green beans with almonds, baby potatoes roasted with garlic and rosemary, some sort of lentil salad, and," he hesitated as he tried to read the label, "queen-ie-o-a? I've personally never heard of it, but it's apparently the new trendy thing that everyone's eating these days. I'm a little afraid, but hey, I'm willing to try anything once. Like that kale stuff you made me last week." He made a face that looked like he was being tortured. "That stuff was awesome. Loved it."

Tessa laughed again. "It's pronounced *keen-wa,* and it happens to be very good *and healthy.* What was wrong with my kale? Everyone I've made it for so far has raved about it."

"Nothing, sweetie. That's what I'm trying to tell you. It was fabulous. The bomb. It was better than—"

"Todd! Todd! You're here!"

"There's my favorite three year old." He grinned, scooping her up in his arms. He swung her around in a circle as she squealed in delight. "I hope you're hungry. I brought you macaroni and cheese and ravioli. And, um, chicken nuggets and French fries. And, well … spaghetti and meatballs, too." He laughed.

"That's too much food," Sophie said, frowning. "I'll get a belly ache."

"Maybe I did bring a little too much."

"Sweetie," Tessa said, "For tonight, you can just pick one of those to eat. We'll save the rest for another time."

"Okay. I'll take ravioli."

"Oh, and for dessert, I have chocolate chip cookies for you, Sophie, and three different kinds of cheesecake for us." Todd smiled, looking at Tessa.

"Yum! Mommy, can I go play?"

"Of course, we'll eat in a little bit." She watched as her daughter ran off to her bedroom. "You're trying to make me fat, aren't you? Is that your plan?"

"Nope. My plan is to spoil you. I know you'll be working hard the next few days with the meeting coming up, so this way you won't have to think about meals. They said you could freeze whatever you don't eat, and I figure you can bring some stuff to work, too.

Maybe Abbott will even give you ten minutes to eat lunch."

Tessa raised her eyebrows as she finished unpacking the bags.

"Five minutes?" he asked.

"Thirty seconds if I'm lucky. I can't wait until this meeting is over. No offense, of course. Without your boss, I'd probably be without a job. The fees from these consultations pay my salary."

"I just wish Abbott treated you better. It's not right. If only there was a way to get that message through to him."

Tessa felt a well of panic rise up. "You're not going to say anything to Mr. Schilling, are you? Please, promise me. I know you mean well. There's only one thing greater than the fees that Mr. Schilling pays and that's Mr. Abbott's enormous ego. If your boss says anything to him about me, he'd kick me out on my ass so hard I wouldn't even see it coming, and I need this job—at least until I find another one. Please, Todd, promise me?"

Taking her hands in his own, he looked at her sadly. "I don't like it, but I promise. Listen, you don't have to worry, Tessa. I know Nicholas Schilling would never let anything bad happen to you."

She wrapped her arms around his neck. "Thank you … for everything. You're so good to me. How'd I get so lucky? Not just for the food, but for the way you care about me … and Sophie."

"I'm the lucky one," he responded, kissing her. "And as for the food, I was kind of selfishly hoping you'd invite me over for another meal. I mean, look at all of this stuff! You can't possibly eat this all by yourself."

She wondered if he realized he could probably get whatever he wanted just by showing her those dimples. "Ah, now I see your true plan," she snickered.

"And? Did it work?" he asked, pulling her in tighter.

Closing her eyes, she pressed her body against his even more. She wanted him so desperately. For weeks they'd waited. They'd been close many times, but she'd always been the one to slow things down. Tonight she felt different. Tonight she felt ready.

"Todd," she whispered. She wanted to let him know this evening would be special ... *so special*. She felt him tense up and pull back. "What's the matter?" she asked.

He looked at her with a serious expression she knew couldn't be good; an expression she dreaded seeing. Had she been misreading all of the signs this entire time? Was the food a parting gift? A pity offering for the poor, single mom to ease his guilt? Were his words of *him being the lucky one* and *wanting to spoil her* just that: only words? What about what he'd just said about hoping she'd invite him back for another meal? He took her hand and led her over to the couch.

28

T his is it, Tessa thought. *This is the part where I find out my perfect guy is not perfect. Poor Sophie. She's going to be devastated, and she's going to blame me. For good reason, too. I'm her mother. It's my job to protect her from getting hurt—to protect both of us.*

Tessa wouldn't look him in the eyes; she couldn't. She didn't want him to see the tears that were starting to form. Todd placed his hands over hers just as one of those tears dropped onto it. He lifted her chin to see her face.

"Why are you crying?" he asked.

"I don't know," she said, "I just ... I–I have a bad feeling."

He embraced her fully with both arms as she sobbed into his shoulder, trembling as years of pent up emotions finally escaped. He held her tight, stroking her hair, allowing her to weep until there were no more tears to shed.

So much for not letting him see you cry, Tessa. "I feel like a fool," she stated, slowly lifting herself off his shoulder. "Me and my crazy emotions. I understand if you want to leave."

"I'm not going anywhere," he replied, rubbing her back. "But I do need to talk to you."

Tessa glanced down and wrung her hands together in her lap, not sure she was ready for whatever he needed to say.

Letting out a hard breath, he looked away for a moment. "I've been wanting to tell you something for a while now, there just never seemed to be a good time."

She glanced his way and waited for more as silence filled the air, but he only leaned his head back into the couch, appearing distressed as he scrubbed his hands over his face. Was he seriously going to pretend breaking up with her was painful to him?

"A good time to tell me what?" she finally asked, not wanting to prolong the inevitable.

At any moment, her daughter could walk into the room asking about dinner or wanting to crawl into

Todd's lap as she'd done so many times before. Would this be the last time Sophie would ever see him? How would she explain his sudden disappearance? Her tears began to flow freely once again.

Shifting his body toward her, he tried to take her hands ... unsuccessfully.

"Tessa, please, don't cry," he began, "it's not like that. Nothing has changed about the way I feel for you. In fact I–I ... ugh, I suck at this."

Furrowing her brow, she studied his face. His expression appeared to be one of adoration and kindness, mixed with fear. Maybe her sisters were right. He was trying to tell her the L word. That had to have been what he'd been trying to tell her the last few weeks. Ben was right. Men really were stupid buffoons. Deciding to take pity on him, she allowed him to take her hands after all.

"It's okay," she said, hoping her smile would put him at ease. "You can tell me."

He took another deep breath and nodded. "All right." His face softened up and his lips curled into a smile to match her own. "As I was saying, when I first walked into Abbott and Associates, I didn't realize that you thought I was someone other than who I am."

Laughing, she shook her head. "Sorry about that. I tend to get a little nervous when I'm in the office by myself. My mom always kept our doors and windows locked once my dad left for work in the morning. Anytime anyone came to the door it was like she was on a covert mission, peeking behind the curtains, trying to decide if it was safe to let them in or not. She had 9-1-1 on speed dial, even though it was only three numbers and not really all that hard to remember. I think her paranoia rubbed off on me a bit."

"Well, it's better to be safe than sorry."

"I'm glad you weren't a murderer or anything ... and even happier for your own sake that I didn't have any pepper spray on me."

"Yeah," Todd cringed, "me too."

"That was such a great day," Tessa added.

"It was, and so was our date," he said, bringing his hand up to caress her cheek. "In fact, that's the night I ... started falling in love with you."

He said it.

"You love me?" she asked. She needed to hear it one more time.

Placing his other hand on her cheek, he brought her face in close. "Yes, Tessa. I never thought it was possible to fall in love so quickly, but there is no doubt about it. I am completely in love with you. I knew it when I realized you cared about me even though you thought I was someone different."

Her eyes filled with tears, as she laughed. "Well, just so you know, I don't usually date guys who are hardened criminals."

Pulling away slowly, he looked her in the eyes. "I know that. What I meant was—"

"Mommy!" Running into the room, Sophie jumped onto the tiny couch landing squarely on the two of them. She snuggled into their laps before saying, "I'm hungry."

"Me, too, actually," Tessa said. "We should probably start eating."

"Sure," Todd said with a hint of disappointment. He helped Sophie down as he stood up, and added, "I don't want to stay too late. I know you have a busy day at work tomorrow, and I've got an early morning meeting myself. However, I do want to finish this conversation ... soon."

She nodded, and he offered her a hand. As she pulled herself up to standing, she wrapped her arms around his neck and quietly told him, "I love you, too."

29

"I haven't had a chance to see him all week," Tessa whispered into the phone to Ava. "It's killing me. Friday night can't come soon enough. I really appreciate you taking Sophie for me this weekend. I have no idea what Todd has planned, but I have a feeling it's something extra special. I do know it has something to do with the conversation we started before Sophie interrupted us. He keeps saying he wants to finish it, and it started with *I love you,* so I can only imagine the rest is going to be even better. Oh that reminds me, can I borrow that dress again? I want to wow him when he comes over."

"Of course. Um ... you don't think he's going to propose, do you?" Ava asked, her excitement radiating through the phone.

"What? No. I don't think we're there yet. At least, I'm not, but I do think we're ready to take the next step. You know ..."

"I know? Oh!" Her sister suddenly laughed, realizing what Tessa was talking about. "Yes, okay. If that's what you want. Is it?"

"It's been a really long time for me," she sighed, "and Todd is the one I've been waiting for. I do love him. Yes, I'm ready."

"Well then, I'm happy to watch Sophie. It's no problem at all. The kids are looking forward to it, especially Jenna."

"Really? I'd have thought Logan would be more excited."

"Oh, he's plenty excited, but Jenna's excited there will be someone else here to entertain Logan all day Saturday. He bugs her non-stop to play with him. I think she's looking forward to the break."

Tessa laughed. "I suppose that's how you and Holly used to feel when I had friends over?"

"I refuse to comment on the grounds that ... um ... well, I just refuse to comment. And what do you mean *used to feel*. Why do you think I jumped at the chance to take Sophie so you could go out with Todd this weekend? We're all excited you have a new playmate."

"What?" she said a little too loudly. She hoped Mr. Abbott wouldn't be showing up in her doorway any second. She paused for a second and heard that he was still on his own phone call. She lowered her voice back down. "Are you saying you just want Todd around so he'll take me off your hands?"

"Of course not. You're an absolute pleasure to have around … All. The. Time."

Tessa scowled without responding. She knew her sister was kidding. Or was she?

"Oh, I'm just teasing. Wow, you really do need some *stress relief.*"

She dropped her voice down to the softest whisper possible. "You have no idea. Especially in the last few days with this meeting coming up today. You know how my boss can be. I've barely gotten any sleep."

"*Tessa!*" Mr. Abbott's voice was so loud she swore she felt the building shake.

"Shit," she groaned. "I've got to go. I'll call you when I get home later … if I survive."

She hung up her phone without waiting for Ava to respond and swiftly walked into her boss' office with a pad of paper and pen, ready for the onslaught of orders. The meeting was scheduled to begin in an hour in their conference room, which was unusual. Mr. Abbott and Mr. Schilling always met downtown. In fact, Nicholas Schilling had never been to the offices of Abbott and Associates before. She gathered from conversations she'd had with Todd that his boss did not have the temper Mr. Abbott had; however, with all that money she imagined he had to be just as self-centered. She wondered how both of their egos would fit in their tiny conference room.

Tessa had gotten to work an hour early. In addition to her professional duties as financial accountant—the job she'd actually been hired to do—she'd assumed that as the only *woman* in the office, her boss would expect that she clean and set up the conference room. Not that he would notice or acknowledge her taking initiative to perform any of these tasks, but she knew had she not done them, he'd find a way to belittle her for missing them. Trying to avoid such a confrontation, she decided to come in early and spend her time vacuuming, dusting, and emptying the trashcan, as he was too cheap to hire a cleaning service to come more than once a month. She set out water pitchers, coffee urns, cups, napkins, tea bags, and anything else she could think of that they might need for morning drinks. She then placed three business folders, complete with reports, papers, and writing utensils on the conference table, one each for Mr. Abbott, Mr. Schilling, and one for Todd, who always accompanied his boss to these meetings. Of course, she'd have to pretend she didn't know him, at least for now. Hopefully she'd be able to keep her secret. It would be tough knowing he was in the same building.

"Are you listening?" Mr. Abbott snarled.

"I'm sorry, sir, I was just remembering that I needed to get the coffee started. Would you mind repeating that?"

"Tessa, do you have any idea how important this meeting is?"

"Yes, sir," she responded, looking confused. After all of the work she put in, how could he even ask her such a question?

He got up from his desk and paced the floor. "Word on the street is that Nicholas has been spending a lot of time out of the office lately. My guess is he's thinking about a new business venture."

"Is that a problem?" Tessa asked, wondering why this was of significance. Was he not allowed to leave his office? And how odd that people kept tabs on his whereabouts.

He stopped pacing and stared at her. "Of course it's a problem. Every day he gets some greedy vultures knocking on his door, wanting him to invest in their hot new idea. I'm Nicholas' accountant. He's never once considered a new business without running it by me first. These early meetings that he's most likely been going to without me are always the most vital when dealing in business proposals. He's always valued my opinion. His lack of contacting me can only mean one thing."

"I'm sorry, I still don't completely understand," Tessa responded.

Mr. Abbott stared at her. She knew that look. It was the warning look to let her know he was about to lose his patience.

"Obviously, it means he's been vetting some new accountant. Someone in the city, someone who can guide him through this new business deal. Why else would he be acting this way? I've suspected for a couple of weeks now that something's been going on. That's why I insisted on having the meeting here at Abbott and Associates. I was able to schedule it with some flaky temp in his office. I wanted to have home field advantage. I had visions of his cronies all ganging up on me up there on the 31st floor of his building. At least if he fires me here, I won't have to do a walk of shame out of there."

"Well, I doubt it's anything like that," she stated confidently.

"How can you say that, Tessa? Do you know something about that office that I don't?" Mr. Abbott stared right at her, right into her face, as if he knew she had inside information ... if he were searching for clues from some great traitor.

"No, of course not," she responded, shifting uncomfortably in her chair. "Mr. Schilling doesn't strike me to be someone who likes to waste time. If he wanted a new accountant, why would he go through the trouble of even having a status meeting? Wouldn't he be more direct, tell you he doesn't need our services anymore, and then let his new accountant take over these consultations?"

"Maybe." Mr. Abbott sunk back into his seat. He suddenly looked smaller, less confident. Tessa almost felt sorry for the guy. *Almost.* "Go on," he said, waving his hand at her. "Make the coffee. I want to go over these numbers one more time before he and that annoying financial guy he drags along everywhere with him get here. And don't forget to put out the scotch and cigars."

"Right," Tessa said, cringing as she walked out the door.

30

Tessa watched from her office window as the limousine pulled in at exactly ten o'clock. *Right on time and arriving in style.* She stood up from her desk and wiped her sweaty palms on her skirt. It was time for her to play receptionist. Walking into the lobby, she waited by the door as the two men approached. The sight of Todd in a suit took her breath away. He looked so handsome. Mr. Schilling, on the other hand, looked exactly as she expected—stodgy and old. If she had to guess, she'd say he was close to seventy. He was also impeccably dressed in a suit and a very nice one at that. She wasn't surprised. With the amount of money he had, he probably had it custom made. Both men held briefcases as they entered through the front door.

"Hello, welcome. I'm Tessa," she said nervously, holding out her hand to Mr. Schilling first, then to Todd.

He winked at her as he held her hand a second longer than he should have. Biting the inside of her cheek to keep from smiling, she darted her eyes away, hoping her face was not too flushed.

With her heart beating way too fast, she continued, "Mr. Abbott is waiting for you both in the conference room. Please, follow me."

Trembling, she walked down the hallway, trying to steady herself with each step.

"Mr. Abbott," she announced as she opened the double doors, "Mr. Schilling and his assistant are here."

"Nicholas, Todd, welcome," Mr. Abbott said, in the same professional voice he used over the telephone. He shook their hands and motioned for them to sit down.

"Can I get anyone anything to drink?" Tessa asked. When they said no, she said a prayer of silent thanks. Her hands were so shaky she certainly would have spilled coffee all over something or someone.

"Thank you, Tessa, that will be all," her boss stated.

Nodding, she closed the doors behind her, taking deep breaths as she made her way back to her office.

"Holy shit," she whispered as she sunk into her chair. She was so out of sorts, even the smallest tasks couldn't keep her attention. She sat alternating between watching the clock on the wall and the birds on the trees outside her window.

The buzz from the intercom on her phone twenty minutes later nearly made her jump out of her seat.

"Yes, sir?" she meekly responded.

"Could you come in here, please?" Mr. Abbott asked.

"Yes, sir," she repeated.

He sounded calm. Oddly calm. She'd never been called into a client meeting before, and she had a bad feeling this wasn't going to go well. Now she could add getting yelled at in front of their biggest client, not to mention her boyfriend, to the list of reasons why she hated her boss. She grabbed the same pad of paper and pen she carried into his office earlier and started her walk of shame toward the conference room.

As she entered, she kept her eyes on her boss, but noticed out of the corner of her eye that the Todd and Mr. Schilling stood to greet her. Mr. Abbott, however, stayed seated and motioned for the two men to sit, without offering her a seat.

"Yes, sir," she said, addressing her boss.

She wanted to look at Todd, but she knew if she did, she wouldn't be able to concentrate on whatever it was Mr. Abbott was about to tell her. Or maybe having a distraction that allowed her to tune out getting yelled at would be a good thing. No, she needed to have all her wits about her right now, even if it meant being the brunt of his temper.

"Tessa," he said, keeping his voice pleasant, "would you mind running off another set of reports? I'm afraid we've had a little mishap." He subtly pointed to a wad of wet paper towels in front of Mr. Schilling.

Having been so nervous when she walked in, she hadn't even noticed. No wonder her boss was being so nice. Old man Schilling had spilled his coffee everywhere, and the last thing her boss probably wanted to do was embarrass him. Although, she was sure that after the meeting was over, she'd get blamed somehow. *Tessa, why didn't you make sure the table was perfectly level?*

"Certainly, sir. Let me get that for you." Scooping up the wet towels, she finished cleaning the area and said, "I'll be right back."

Within minutes, she knocked on the conference room door and returned carrying a new folder for their wealthiest client.

"Here you are, Mr. Schilling," she said, as she placed the papers in front of him. "Can I get you anything else, sir? More coffee?"

"Tessa," Mr. Abbott said, now sounding a little annoyed, "that's not Mr. Schilling." He looked over to Todd and added, "I'm so sorry, Nicholas. My assistant appears to be a bit confused."

Not Mr. Schilling? What the hell was going on here?
She gazed at the old man she believed to be Mr. Schilling, but he only stared back at her with a blank look on his face, before shifting her attention to Todd. Remorse filled his eyes as he met hers, before she quickly glanced away.

Grasping the table in hopes of keeping the room from swaying, she tried to calm her racing heart. Looking at Mr. Abbott, she softly said, "Of course." She then turned her head back to the man she had known to be Todd for the last six weeks and coldly stated, "Please forgive me, Mr. Schilling."

"Tessa, please," he started as he rose from his chair, "I'm so sorry. I didn't mean for you to find out this way. You have to believe me."

"No," she said, backing away from him as he reached his arm out to her. "No."

"Please, I tried to tell—"

She never heard the rest as she raced out of the conference room, grabbed her belongings, and ran out of the office, ignoring Nicholas' excuses and pleas to wait.

31

Ava sighed into the phone. "What do you mean you quit your job?"

Tessa paced back and forth in her tiny kitchen, clutching her cell phone in one hand and a cup of tea in the other, explaining the events that transpired that morning to her oldest sister. Despite being home for thirty minutes already, her body was still trembling. She placed the tea on the table, unable to keep it steady with just one hand.

After learning the truth, she bolted. She realized that probably wasn't the most rational decision, but there was no way she could possibly stay there in the building with *him* in the conference room down the hall. Nor could she continue to work on his files. *Who the hell was he anyway?* At some point she'd have to return to retrieve her personal belongings: a couple of plants, a framed photo of Sophie, a mug, and some hand cream. Come to think of it, nothing there was really all that important. She had plenty of other pictures of Sophie, and the plants were half dead.

"Well, I didn't quit exactly," Tessa explained. "I just ran out ... with the intention of never returning. Not that Mr. Abbott would let me return to work anyway. I'm sure I completely tarnished his *good name.*"

"Tessa, just calm down for a moment. Have you spoken to Todd?"

"You mean Nicholas? At least I think it's Nicholas, I can't keep up these days. I mean he could be a George or a Luke for all I know."

Ava sighed again. "Yes, I'm talking about Nicholas. Have you spoken to him?"

Tea splattered over the sides of her cup as she tried to take a tiny sip. Nicholas, Todd, or whoever the hell he was had texted her six times since she'd left the office and left three voicemails, all pleading with her to talk to him. She'd ignored them all. At least he had the decency not to show up at her door. Not yet at least. What would she tell Sophie when she picked her up from daycare later? That the man she'd come to care so much for wouldn't be coming by anymore? She wasn't prepared to mend two broken hearts.

"No, I haven't spoken to him," Tessa replied. "And if he doesn't stop trying to call and text, I'm going to change my number. He's getting dangerously close to me filing a harassment charge."

"I'm just thinking maybe you need to give him a chance to explain," Ava told her.

"The same way I gave Scott a chance? Do you see a trend here, Ava? Men suck. I'm seriously beginning to think you and Holly got the last two good ones."

"I know you're hurting, and I don't blame you for being completely furious. All I'm saying is it's possible he had a good reason for hiding his true identity."

Tessa laughed. "A good reason? Next you're going to tell me he's some CIA operative. Ooh, maybe I was dating James Bond. Do you think he goes by a code name like 007? Or maybe he's really a superhero like Batman or something. Do you think after he leaves me, he changes into his tights and cape and fights crime? But what if he's really a villain and uses his power for evil and not good? That would really suck."

She waited for Ava's response, which as expected was silence. So she continued, "Do you hear how ridiculous you sound, Av? What good is a relationship if it starts off based on a lie? I'll tell you how good it is. It's no good."

"Are you finished?" Ava asked. Tessa could hear the impatience growing in her voice.

"Yes."

"Good. Now listen to me. First of all, you told me more than once he had started to try to tell you something and stopped. For whatever reason, he wanted to tell you, but couldn't."

"So he's a liar and a coward," she responded. "Keep going. So far, your argument is not very convincing."

"You're supposed to be listening," her sister told her. "Second, I know I don't need to remind you how Max and I started out. He wasn't telling me the truth either at the beginning, and I gave him a second chance."

Tessa shook her head. It was just like her sister to take Nicholas' side. She always did believe in fairy tale endings. But was she forgetting about the other guy in her life at the time? That artist guy, Thomas? Not all guys deserved second chances. Now probably wasn't the best time to bring him up, not after all these years.

"Your circumstances were completely different. Max wasn't lying about his identity. He was lying about a situation. And he wasn't even lying. He was protecting you from getting your heart broken. It was quite chivalrous when you think about it. Apples and oranges, Ava. Anyway, I'm just glad I found out about Nicholas before I ..."

Reaching for the tissue from the box she had behind her on the counter, she wiped her eyes. She really did love Todd. At least she loved the person she thought was Todd. Now she didn't know who this person was. Not at all. The last several weeks had been spent with a complete stranger. She knew he was too good to be true. *She should have listened to her instincts. That wall was there for a reason.*

"... before I showed him just how much I loved him," she quietly continued.

Ava was silent for a moment. "I'm so sorry, sweetie."

"And now, I'm out of a job," she added.

"What are you going to do?" her sister asked.

Rentals in Forest Hills were in high demand with the university so close. She'd lucked out with her apartment. Even though it had two tiny bedrooms, she paid the going rate for a one-bedroom, since it technically was, without the flimsy dividing wall between her and Sophie's rooms. Despite the lack of space, the place was perfect. It would be foolish for her to move. Of course, without a job, she may not have a choice. The rent would be due soon. She wondered if Ava was already wondering how she would house her youngest sister and niece if they got kicked out of their apartment.

"I have no idea," Tessa whispered, as tears continued to roll down her cheeks.

32

"**M**ama, is Todd coming over tonight?"
Despite the ominous cloud lingering over Tessa, the sun shone brightly as she pulled her car into the parking lot of Sophie's daycare Monday morning. Turning off the ignition, she ran her hands over her face and through her hair, wondering when and how to break the news to her daughter they wouldn't be seeing the man they had only known as Todd ever again.

Upon both of her sisters' advice, Sophie stayed the weekend with Ava, Max, and the kids. Tessa reluctantly agreed at first. Part of her selfishly wanted to spend the weekend curled up with her daughter, both to take in her sweet cuddles and smells and to also give her the support she may need, but another part of her looked at her innocent and happy face and thought, *What harm is there in waiting a few days to tell her?*

She was glad she took their advice. After dropping Sophie off, Tessa sat in her apartment and listened as Nicholas knocked on her door, asking her to open up so they could talk. Pounded and pleaded was more like it. She was surprised none of the neighbors had called the police. She supposed it was because they were used to seeing him around so much. That, and she wasn't exactly living in the best neighborhood. Loud sounds from the hallway were nothing out of the ordinary.

Sitting in silence on her couch, knees tucked tightly into chest and tears streaming down her face, she refused to give even the slightest hint she was home. Eventually, the pounding softened up, and when she was sure the coast was clear, she opened her door to find a sealed envelope attached to a bouquet of pink flowers, all of which she promptly threw into the hallway trash chute. She wasn't interested in reading his excuses.

Early the next day, he showed up with the same routine. Thankfully, he appeared to have taken the hint, as that was his last visit. His calls and texts had finally stopped as well.

Other than dealing with Nicholas, Tessa spent a decent amount of time talking with Holly; although, she was fairly certain Ava was the mastermind behind it all. She knew exactly how their conversation went. *Try to have her over for the afternoon, and get her to stay for dinner. If she refuses, check in with her at least once every hour. You could always stop by her place, too. Say you were in the area shopping or something, so it seems less obvious. Whatever you do, don't let her just sit around to wallow in her own self-pity.*

She knew they meant well, but Holly didn't exactly *do* subtle. When she stopped over unannounced after her third hourly call to borrow a teaspoon of vanilla for baking, Tessa knew something was up.

First of all, Holly didn't bake. Second, neither did Tessa, and third, on the off chance that Holly *was* actually going to try her hand at some sort of dessert, why would she drive out of her way to Tessa's apartment to borrow vanilla that she knew her sister most likely wouldn't have, when Holly had a grocery store in her own neighborhood? It made no logical sense.

"Hey, Tessa, I knew you'd be feeling like crap so I brought you some booze."

Now that would have worked much better with the same amount of subtlety. Plus, they could have stayed in her apartment for hours, pulled out some board games, or watched some goofy movie, of the non-romantic variety, of course. Tessa made a mental note to talk to Holly about the art of sisterly care when she was feeling better.

Still, one good thing did come out of the weekend. She took Holly up on her lunch offer Sunday afternoon. If anything, Ben would be home, and she knew he would cheer her up. Her pseudo-big brother always seemed to know just what to say. Tessa was right, but it wasn't the pep talk she was expecting. In speaking with him, she found out that the plant he managed was hiring a full-time bookkeeper. It wasn't the exact job she was hoping to get, but it would pay the bills, and the benefits were better than what she'd had at Abbott's place. Just as soon as she dropped Sophie off, she'd planned on heading over to fill out the application. Ben mentioned they'd already had several applicants, and unfortunately, while he could put in a good word, the accounting department was out of his jurisdiction. Still, she hoped that her experience, as well as her connections to both Ben and her father, who had worked there almost his entire adult life before retiring, would be enough of a boost to put her ahead of the pack. It was worth a shot at least.

"Mama?" the sweet voice asked again from the back seat.

"What's that, honey?"

"I said, when am I going to see Todd? I miss him. He's funny. He makes me laugh."

"Oh, well, I'm not sure." Tessa hated having to give such vague answers to her daughter. It would be so easy for her to say he was on a business trip, busy at work, or to make up some other story, but then she'd be just adding to the lies herself. No, she refused to add to his pile of deceit. At the same time, she wasn't prepared to have a conversation about what happened right there in the car. They did, however, need to talk about it today, after she picked her up. Sophie obviously missed him and would keep asking until she addressed the issue. She just needed more time to prepare. How do you have that type of conversation with a three year old anyway?

"Can we call him later to see if he wants to meet us at the playground?" she asked.

So innocent. Look what you've done. She doesn't deserve this. "We'll talk about it later," Tessa answered with a shaky voice. "Right now, though, we better get inside, or you'll be late for circle time. I know that's your favorite."

"Okay, Mama."

33

The number on the caller ID surprised her. She hadn't expected him to call her today. Or at all when it came right down to it. Maybe he wasn't done yelling at her. Pulling into an empty spot at the plastics plant parking lot, she hoped this wouldn't take long. The bookkeeper's job wasn't going to be around much longer. If she just ignored the call, it would go to voicemail, but he'd only call back again ... and again. He didn't like being snubbed. Might as well get this over with.

"Hello?" she answered with a certain level of aggravation.

The old Tessa would have been completely intimidated. The new Tessa didn't give a shit. Let him yell. She could always hang up, after giving him a few choice words of her own, of course. On second thought, she might need him for a job recommendation. Plan B: Get new job first, then tell off old asshole boss. Yes, she liked that idea, but for now, she needed to hear him out.

"Tessa?" the voice asked. It was Mr. Abbott all right, minus his usual belligerent tone. He sounded almost kind. Almost.

"Yes," she replied.

"I know you had a rough day on Thursday." He stopped, as if trying to figure out how to form the words. "I'm ... sorry about that."

Pulling the phone away from her ear, she checked the caller ID again. The voice sounded familiar, but the words coming out of his mouth were completely foreign. At least coming from him. *He's up to something. Is this the calm before the storm?*

"Tessa? Are you there?"

Yes, that was Mr. Abbott on the phone. Apologizing with empathy. Either she was dreaming, or he was highly medicated. She opted for the latter option.

"I'm here," she said, not quite sure how to respond to his prior comment.

"I'm glad you took the day off on Friday to rest. You deserved a day to yourself after working so hard.

We all need a day off now and again. I always say that."

He does? When does he always say that? Tessa blinked several times to help process his words. *Just what kind of medication was he taking?*

"So now that you've had a nice three day weekend, I hope you're feeling refreshed."

"Um, okay." She would have said more, but she was at a loss for words. Was this his plan? Make her speechless, then deliver the final blow?

"Anyway, I was calling to see what time you'd be coming in this morning. You're usually here by now. I was just making sure everything is okay."

Tessa squinted her eyes as if trying to focus on the words. Maybe they would make more sense that way. It didn't work. It was time for her to go for a more direct approach. "I'm fine, but I assumed I was fired. I wasn't planning on coming back."

"Fired? Don't be ridiculous." Mr. Abbott laughed nervously. It was a scary sound she'd never heard come out of her boss before. He gathered himself and continued, "No, no, not at all. Nicholas was very impressed with your work. In fact, he seemed very upset that you ran out. He couldn't stop talking about what an asset you were to the firm. We met again on Friday, actually, to continue our discussion."

"Interesting," she said, examining her nails, while trying to figure out where the conversation was going.

"Tessa," Mr. Abbott said, clearly struggling to get the words out, "I've been going over my books. I've had a very good year, thanks in great part to your efforts. I would like to offer you a raise ... with a bonus ... as a token of my appreciation."

She stopped what she was doing. Now she knew he was up to something. *Token of his appreciation?* Since when did her boss—her former boss—show appreciation? Plus, Mr. Abbott didn't need to *go over his books.* He was an accountant. He knew exactly what his profit margin was every second of every day, and it was never high enough. *Never.* He hadn't ever offered her a raise or a cash bonus. At most, he *might* bring her out to some fancy dinner, and then complain something was wrong with his entree so the restaurant would give it to him for free. Come to think of it, he'd never taken her out for a meal, either. That scenario, while most likely accurate, was really just all in her head. No, Mr. Abbott did not freely part with money or compliments.

"I thought Mr. Schilling was looking for a new accountant."

While the topic of a pay increase and bonus certainly intrigued her, she was more interested in digging for further information concerning Nicholas. She cringed as his nervous laugh resurfaced. Holding the phone away from her ear, she waited for the horrid noise to end.

He cleared his throat and continued, "It was all a misunderstanding. It seems he was out of the office most of the time for personal reasons. I was worrying for nothing. He's more than pleased with our services and might even increase the frequency of our projections."

"Is that so?" she asked.

"Well, yes. That's what I've been trying to tell you. He's even agreed to increase my fee as long as you—"

She let out a heavy sigh. So that's why he was calling. It all made perfect sense now. Nicholas was behind all of this, not Mr. Abbott. He was using his money to buy her.

"—as long as I stay on at Abbott and Associates? I appreciate the offer, sir, but I can't accept it."

"But, Tessa, please, hear me out, I'm authorized to pay you—"

She ended the call before she could hear the amount and went inside Ben's plant to apply for the bookkeeping job, with or without a referral from her former boss.

34

Ava volunteered to watch Sophie, *yet again,* so Tessa could show Ben and Holly her appreciation for helping her get her new job. She wanted to take them out to eat, but couldn't afford it. Instead, she offered to cook them dinner at their house, and figured it would be easier if she were kid-free. As always, she felt bad, especially since Max was home for once, but Ava insisted. Securing the bookkeeping job at Ben's plant was a huge relief ... *for everyone.* She would offer to watch Jenna and Logan for the weekend the next time Max was home. They deserved it, and there was much to thank them for as well.

"Have I told you in the last ten minutes how grateful I am, Ben?" Tessa asked, as they all sat in her oldest sister's living room.

"Really, it's not necessary. I told you, I had nothing to do with it other than letting you know the job was open. The rest was all you."

"I know, but the job wasn't even advertised. All of the candidates were from within. I wouldn't have even known about the position if it wasn't for you. I guess that means I won't be making any friends there. I imagine there will be a lot of pissed off applicants."

"Maybe. I don't get involved in office politics. Well, it's not entirely by choice. They don't let the plant workers anywhere near that accounting office, even us manager types, although they do pretend to be slightly nicer to us, but it's all an act. I'm sure after they talk to me, they go in the restroom to hose off the best they can. You'd think we had the plague or something. You'll see once you start working there. It's a *them versus us* mentality."

"I thought you ran the place," Max stated.

"No," Ben corrected. "I run the plant. The administrative area, which includes bookkeeping, H.R., and all of the other stuff where you don't get your hands dirty, is totally separate. We're peons to them."

"That's ridiculous," Tessa stated. "Now I fully intend to mingle with you while I'm there, just to see their reaction." She rubbed her palms together and smirked. "Maybe I'll even shake your hand in front of them and wipe it on their desks. You know, since no one will be my friend anyway."

"You want to keep this new job, don't you?" Holly asked.

"Oh, okay, I'll behave," Tessa muttered, looking like a kid who was just scolded. "You ruin all my fun."

"Well, I never was the fun sister. Isn't that what you always say?" Holly flashed a smile and rolled her eyes.

"Hey, would you look at the time," Tessa said, finishing the water Ava had offered her in a single gulp. "We should get going before I change my mind." She gave Holly a peck on the cheek and smiled. "Let me go find my daughter. I'll be right back."

Giggles and squeals of delight led Tessa directly to Sophie, who was buried under a mound of blankets and pillows in the playroom. Apparently, the tent she and her cousin Logan had tried to build had collapsed on top on them—a result that appeared to be far more fun than the intended plan.

Standing in the doorway for a moment, Tessa just stood listening and watching, her heart smiling at the sounds coming from the room.

Sometimes, friendships end. Kind of like how you don't really talk to Anna anymore. It doesn't mean Todd doesn't care about you, and I promise it wasn't anything you did wrong. I know you'll miss him, and that's okay. I know he misses you, too. The words had been so difficult to say to Sophie the other day, and while she seemed to understand, she hadn't been her cheerful self since … until this evening.

"Now where are Sophie and Logan?" Tessa asked, pretending not to have a clue as to their whereabouts as she walked into the playroom. "I could have sworn they were in here, but all I see is a pile of pillows."

Her words only made the two toddlers giggle even louder.

"My, my," she continued, walking toward the puffed up mound, "these are some very noisy pillows, and they look very comfortable, too." Stretching her arms out, she yawned a loud, over-exaggerated yawn. "Oh, boy, am I tired. I think I'll just lie down right here on this nice comfy stack of cushions." She lightly put her foot on top to add just the slightest amount of pressure.

"No!" Sophie and Logan yelled, still giggling, as their little bodies sprung out, tossing pillows everywhere.

"Oh, there you are." Tessa laughed, scooping her daughter up in her arms to sprinkle her nose with tiny kisses. "I'm getting ready to go out. You'll be good for Aunt Ava and Uncle Max, right?"

"Yes, Mommy."

She gave Sophie one more kiss, and one to Logan as well before leaving the room.

"I take it everything's okay in there?" Ava asked when Tessa returned.

"Oh yeah," she replied, smiling. "They're just doing a bit of re-decorating for you."

"Well, you know, it saves me a bundle on hiring a professional. Now go, and enjoy your dinner."

Tessa thanked her sister and brother-in-law and headed outside where Ben and Holly waited for her by their car.

35

Tessa chopped vegetables while soft music played in the background, taking an occasional sip of wine as she worked.

"Are you sure I can't help you?" her sister asked, pacing the floor.

"Nope. What's with you anyway? You're acting strange."

"Nothing. I'm just not used to having someone else doing the work in my kitchen while I hang out and do nothing."

"Stop looking like I'm torturing you. You should be enjoying this. I've got everything under control. In fact," she said, adding the colorful array of peppers, onions, and mushrooms to the skillet, "this will be ready in another ten minutes or so."

"I can't wait. It smells amazing," Ben said, entering the kitchen. Using his fingers, he picked a tomato out of the salad, and popped it into his mouth. "So how are you doing, Tessa? Feeling okay? Would you like a little more wine?"

"I'm good, thanks." She turned around to look at him. Now he was acting odd. What was going on?

"Holly?" he asked. "Can I talk to you for a second?"

"Sure."

Tessa waited until they both left the kitchen before sneaking over to the doorway to where she could hear them whispering:

" *When are you going to tell her?* "

"*I don't know. I was hoping you would tell her.* "

"*No, you're her sister. You should tell her.* "

"*I know, but she seems to listen to you more. Maybe it should be you.* "

Shutting off the burner, she walked into the dining room. "Tell me what?" she asked. She looked at the table. Earlier, she had set it with three place settings, but now it was set for only two. "What's going on?"

Holly looked to Ben before saying to her, "Don't get mad."

Tessa glared back at her. Didn't she realize that when people said *don't get mad*, the first instinct they had was to get mad?

"Why would I?" she asked, trying to keep her voice calm.

Why wasn't Holly answering her? Hesitation was never a good sign. Deciding her sister was taking way too long to respond, she turned around and walked toward the front door. Let them fix their own damn dinner. She swung the door open to leave. That's when she saw *him*, one hand up as if about to knock, the other holding a small bouquet of pink daisies. *Damn it.*

"What are you doing here?" she demanded. Spinning back around, she glared at her sister and brother-in-law, her body filling with rage. *Don't get mad?* No, she wasn't mad, she was fuming. "What is he doing here, Hol?" she demanded again, louder this time.

"Tessa," Holly said, walking over to her sister. She lightly grabbed her arm and pulled her into her hallway away from the men. "He called Ava," she said in a whispered tone, "to explain ... and plead. He just wants a chance to talk to you and didn't know how else to make it happen."

"I'm leaving." She tried to pull her arm away, but her sister tightened her grasp.

"Look at me. You know Ava would never allow anyone to hurt you or Sophie. None of us would. He's a good guy, Tess. He just made a bad decision, and he feels horrible about it. Ava talked to him for over an hour. And after they hung up, he called Ben ... who gave him hell, by the way. Ava apparently did as well. We're not saying he didn't deserve it."

"Hell yeah, he deserved it," Tessa said, relaxing her arm a bit. "Why should I listen to him? Just why should I give him a chance to explain?"

"Do remember a few years back, when I thought I couldn't have Ben?"

She nodded. She remembered it well, like it was yesterday. Holly and Ben had been so in love with each other. Problem was, there was another woman. A woman he didn't belong with. It broke Holly's heart. She had no choice but to cut him out of her life completely. She didn't want to speak, see, or even know of his existence.

"Yes," she responded.

"And do you remember what you did?" Holly asked.

Tessa sighed. Of course she remembered. She surprised Holly with a meeting between the two of them so they could hash it out. The next thing she knew, they were back together and madly in love.

"Okay," she agreed, "I'll hear him out ... but only if you and Ben agree to stay close by."

Holly smiled, bringing her back into the dining room. "We'll be just over there in the kitchen," she said.

Tessa nodded.

Leaning in close to give her a kiss on the cheek, Holly whispered, "Consider the favor repaid." She grabbed Ben's hand.

36

Tessa sat at Holly's dining room table, arms crossed, waiting as Nicholas gulped water.

"Well?" she finally asked, growing increasingly impatient. "I don't get it. For days you've been calling and texting. You even showed up at my apartment twice begging for a chance to talk to me. I know you're responsible for Abbott's odd behavior. That man actually apologized to me. *Apologized!* He's never said he's sorry to anyone *ever*, and I don't even want to discuss the raise and bonus you put him up to—which I didn't accept, as I'm sure you know. And I just found out you called my sister *and* my brother-in-law, who by the way is one of the finest examples of a man you will ever meet. You should really take lessons from him. Then, you came all the way here, obviously hoping you'd get a chance to talk to me. Well, here I am, and now you're just going to sit there, say nothing, and drink water?"

"Vodka would work better," he responded with a half-smile. "Especially since you seem like you're about to bite my head off. Kind of started actually."

"Wow, starting right off with a compliment. Smart move."

"I'm a little nervous. You have that effect on me, you know.

"Why don't you start by telling me why you lied?" She sat back in her chair, enjoying the fact that she was in control of the conversation. *Let him be uncomfortable.* She'd hear what he had to say, but she wouldn't let him get into her heart. Not this time.

"For the record," Nicholas started, "I never lied. I just never corrected you when—"

"Okay, I've heard enough." She pushed back her chair and started to walk toward the front door.

"Wait, please!" he begged, running after her. He placed his hand on her shoulder, and she reluctantly stopped and faced him. "You're absolutely, right," he continued. "I totally lied to you, and it was inexcusable. I'm sincerely sorry. I truly am."

"That's a start," she said.

"Will you come sit back down with me? I just want a chance to explain … why I lied."

Turning her head toward Ben and Holly, who were now standing in the doorway, she nodded to let them know everything was under control. They disappeared back into the kitchen, and she slowly walked over to the table to return to her seat.

"Thank you," he said, and sat down as well, looking slightly relieved. "You have to believe me when I tell you it doesn't change the way I feel about you one bit." His eyes met hers, pleading with her as he spoke. "I love you, Tessa, and you may think you fell in love with Todd, but you didn't. Todd is a sixty-seven year old man with high-blood pressure and arthritis in his right knee. I don't think you're actually in love with him. The guy you fell in love with is sitting across from you right now. I'm still the same guy. My name is just Nicholas. Nick really. I'm a regular guy who went to Forest Hills University and played guitar every Friday night at O'Grady's just like I told you. I even flipped burgers right out of school. And then, just like I explained on our first date, I was at the right place at the right time. All of that was true. I just didn't finish the story."

"You mean the little inconsequential part about how being in the right place at the right time resulted in you becoming the actual multi-millionaire instead of the financial assistant for the multi-millionaire," Tessa said, twisting her napkin in her lap as she spoke. Luckily it was cloth, or there would be a pile of tiny paper shreds on the floor by now.

Nicholas nodded. "Yes."

"But why didn't you tell me who you were when you first came into the office?"

"At first I just assumed you knew who I was."

"No, I had no idea," Tessa replied. "To be honest, you looked pretty shady. Remember? I was ready to call the cops on you. You were a mess."

"Right," he said, trying desperately to get the last drops of water out of his glass from between the ice cubes, before placing it back down on the table. "I had taken the red-eye back from London that day. And, after I landed, I wanted to catch up on some work before heading home to clean up. My administrative assistant was on leave, and I was worried my office would be in complete shambles. When I got to work that morning my desk was a disaster, but there was a note you'd called and were looking for the statements. I was anxious to have an update from Steve—Mr. Abbott—since we missed our original meeting, so I grabbed what I had and ran the statements over to you. It wasn't until we were on our date that I realized you had no idea of my true identity."

"And yet, you never corrected me, even weeks later," Tessa noted, tossing the napkin on the table in order to pick up her own water glass.

"I wanted to tell you, and I tried to, several times, actually. Every time I started, something kept stopping me."

"If you really wanted me to know, you would have found a way."

"You're right," he said, looking away for a moment. "The truth is, I was afraid."

"Of what?" she asked, studying his face. He seemed pained. Was it from sitting here with her or his admission of being scared?

Closing his eyes for a moment as if knowing he had only one chance to say the right words, he began, "When I first realized what had happened, I already knew there was something incredibly special about you. At the same time, I wasn't completely sure how you felt about me. I was afraid if you realized I was Nicholas instead of Todd, I would never find out."

"I don't understand."

He sighed. "I know this is going to sound ridiculous and probably incredibly self-centered, but as Nicholas Schilling I never know if people are really sincere when they appear to like me. Do they like me for me? Or do they like me for my money? It's always a question that lingers in the back of my mind, and as a result, I've never been able to have a true relationship since becoming wealthy. My mother says I build walls."

Tessa raised her eyebrows. *You've got to be kidding me.*

He continued, "So, when you thought I was Todd, and you still enjoyed my company, it was something I hadn't felt since college. Something I had longed to experience. It was kind of nice being *just* Todd."

"It was nice being a sixty-seven-year-old guy with high blood pressure and arthritis?"

"No, it was nice being liked as just a regular guy. Not as Nicholas Schilling, multi-millionaire. Not to sound arrogant, but I get a lot of attention from women once they find out how much money I have."

"Yes, that does sound arrogant."

"Told you. Yet, the sad truth is, none of those woman are worth talking to. Or if they were, I'd never know it. I've met so many who are only interested in me for what I have. It's become nearly impossible for me to tell the difference anymore. I'd pretty much stopped dating all together. That's why when you came along everything was so different. You had no idea who I was. You thought I was a financial assistant, and you liked me for me. Nothing more. That meant everything. I knew I had to tell you, but as time passed, my fear became more visceral—gut wrenching, to be honest. I knew I loved you, and how do you tell the person you love the most in this world you've been lying to them?"

"You just tell them," Tessa said, feeling the sting of tears starting to appear. "Yeah, I would have been pissed, but at least I wouldn't have been standing in front of my boss looking like an idiot, and we would have had a chance to talk things out ... just the two of us."

"I know," he replied, tears forming in his eyes as well. "I never intended for any of that to happen at your office. Looking back, I wish I had scheduled that meeting somewhere else. I wish I had done a lot of things differently. I honestly just thought it would be a good excuse to see you. I was being selfish, and you're the one who paid for it in the end. I know you probably don't believe me, but I did intend to tell you last weekend, no matter what. It's why I wanted to take you out. I knew there would be no distractions or interruptions. And while I also knew there was a chance it would be the end for us, I was sincerely hoping—praying, really—I could convince you how much I truly love you and how sorry I am.

"I trusted you," she said, tears flowing down her face, "I trusted you with my daughter, and I trusted you with my heart. I loved you. I mean, I loved Todd. *Shit.* I don't even know who I fell in love with."

"You fell in love with *me*, Tessa. *Me*. For the true person I am, not for the things I can afford. I'm still that same person. I just have a different name, and I love you more than I can possibly express sitting here at this table. You *and* Sophie. You both mean everything to me. I know I probably don't deserve a second chance, but I want to start over ... with you, and if you feel comfortable, with Sophie, too. We'll take things slow; get to know each other all over again. I promise never to lie to you ever again. I'm so sorry."

She shook her head, looking down.

"Tessa, please, I'm so lost without you."

"Are you really the same person?" she asked, glancing up at him through her tears. The man sitting across the table from her had the same sparkling eyes, the same dark hair, and the same lips that now curved back into a smile revealing the dimples she'd traced with her fingers so many times. He even had the same creases in his forehead as he raised his eyebrows in hopes of getting her to agree.

Nicholas nodded, taking her hands in his own. "I'm right here," he said, gazing intently at her. "And I'm not going anywhere. You have my word."

"**I** see the laundry elves didn't come while I was out," Ava mumbled as she and Ryan entered the house.

"What, Mama?" he asked with a confused expression on his face.

"Nothing, sweetie. Why don't you go play for a little bit while I put all this away and figure out what we're going to do today?" How she wished she could drop her son off at Mrs. Connelly's for a few hours again. Between the impromptu late night with her sisters, an old dog who decided at four in the morning he suddenly had to get let out, having extra mouths to feed at breakfast, and having to drive Logan and Jenna to school, Ava felt like she'd already put in a full day. At least Holly helped get Tessa home. Now she had stuff to do around the house while entertaining her youngest child who unfortunately gave up napping long ago. *Naps.* What a concept. Ava would gladly take one. Who was the genius that decided naps shouldn't be a forever thing? Unfortunately, her sitter wasn't available today, not that Ava would take him to her anyway. She was still feeling a little guilty over the fact that Ryan had put in extra time there yesterday.

"This laundry is not going to fold itself," she reminded herself out loud, staring at the pile of clothing in hopes that some sort of telekinesis might kick in. Was she imagining things, or had the number of items in the basket increased since last night? She grabbed a sweatshirt off the top and began the arduous task, stacking each piece according to its owner.

Thirty minutes later, she found last weekend's *Forest Hills Times* underneath it all. Collapsing on the couch, she skimmed through the first section, making her way to the only news that really mattered to her: Arts and Entertainment.

"No way," she whispered to herself. "I didn't know that was coming to town." She checked her watch and stretched her neck to take a peek into the playroom. Ryan was sitting on the floor quietly coloring. Of her three children, he was the most like his mama, choosing to draw or color over any other activity. He was still a bit young for the Museum of Fine Arts, but on the other hand, he might get a kick out of seeing some of the paintings and sculptures. Besides, it wasn't like she was planning on spending hours there walking through the massive building. She was interested only in this particular show. It wasn't everyday a Julien Henri exhibit came to town. She glanced back down at the article. This week only and the closest stop on his tour.

Ava looked at the piles of folded laundry to be put away and thought about everything on her to-do list for the day. It was the same as always, really: errands, cooking, cleaning, and kids.

"Oh screw it," she said to herself, getting up. "When do I ever do anything for myself?" She tore out the info for the exhibit and walked into the playroom. "Ryan, honey, come on. We're going back out."

Ryan seemed just as enthralled with the paintings at the exhibit as Ava. Well, perhaps enthralled was a bit of a stretch for a three year old. He seemed to have moderate interest. Okay—he wasn't complaining about being dragged around an art museum. Not yet at least. And there was certainly plenty to look at in the exhibit. Julien Henri was a master of his craft. After studying his work while Ava was a student at

Wolfenson College, he'd become one of her favorite artists, second only to her true favorite, Claude Monet. Henri's love of impressionism and use of Monet's techniques were more than evident in his work. In fact, were it not for Henri's distinguishing signature, experts might argue that Monet himself painted some of the pieces now hanging on display. However, Henri was not simply a Monet copycat artist like so many others were. On the contrary, Henri was a talented painter who saw a modern world through impressionist eyes. He deserved every bit of the critical acclaim he'd received during his career.

Back in the day, Ava had tried desperately to get a Julien Henri piece in her gallery, but they were way beyond her reach. Most were just simply not for sale, and if they were, they sold through big auction houses, not small town galleries. She hadn't seen an original Henri painting in years and was completely mesmerized by this incredible collection.

Grabbing Ryan's hand, she walked over to the bench in the center of the room to sit. There was only one way to truly view an exhibit such as this one, and they were lucky it was a quiet Wednesday morning in the museum. Had it been a weekend, they would never have been able to just sit and soak up the view. After pointing out some of the nuances of each of the paintings—clearly all lost on her young son—Ava was content to relax in silence while looking around the room. She found herself getting lost in each piece, imagining Henri in his studio, brush in hand, as he created each work. What were his inspirations? How long did each painting take? Did he struggle with light and shadows as she often did when painting? Most importantly, why didn't she come here to the museum on a regular basis? Every second that passed left her feeling more and more relaxed.

A group of chatty teenagers, students on a school trip presumably, interrupted her thoughts as they filled the room, blocking her view.

She sighed loudly. So much for her stress-free morning.

"I guess that's our cue, buddy." When she looked over to where Ryan had been sitting, she discovered he was no longer there. "Ryan?" she called out, searching the room, trying to see through the crowd. Her heart raced as she jumped up and pushed people aside in a panic, continuing to call out his name. He was *just* here. *Wasn't he?* How long had she been zoned out?

"Ryan?"

"*Ryan!*"

About the Author

Karen Pokras writes adult contemporary and middle grade fiction under the names Karen Pokras and Karen Pokras Toz. Her books have won several awards including two Readers' Favorite Book Awards, the Grand Prize in the Purple Dragonfly Book Awards, as well as placing first for two Global E-Book Awards for Pre-Teen Literature. A native of Connecticut, Karen now lives outside of Philadelphia with her family. For more information, visit www.karenpokras.com and www.karentoz.com

I have to admit I have a soft spot for Tessa. Many years ago, under a different set of circumstances, I found myself working for my own "Steven Abbott." No, I wasn't swept away by a millionaire, but I am quite content with my present day life. And so, I need to send a very special thank you to my family and friends. Without you cheering me on, I might not be where I am today, and for that, I am eternally grateful. As for this book, there are many who played a role in helping bring this book to life, starting with my fabulous beta readers, Kathie and Megan. They are my first eyes and the ones who make me think the most. Also fabulous is my editor, Melissa Ringsted, to whom I owe more thanks to than I can possibly write here. To the team at Najla Qamber Designs, thank you to you as well. The covers you created for this series are beyond my expectations.

And to my readers—I can't say this enough! Thank you, so much for believing in me and for your overwhelming support. Feel free to drop me a line - **I love hearing from you!**

karenpokrasauthor@gmail.com

Whispered Wishes Series:
Book 1: Ava's Wishes
Book 2: Holly's Wishes
Book 3: Tessa's Wishes
Book 4: Woven Wishes
Merry Wishes: A Whispered Wishes Novella

Chasing Invisible (Karen Pokras Toz)

Books for Children 7-12 (Karen Pokras Toz)
Nate Rocks the World
Nate Rocks the Boat
Nate Rocks the School
Nate Rocks the City
Millicent Marie Is Not My Name
Pie and Other Brilliant Ideas